NICKAJACK

Robert J. Conley

D1455346

BANTAM BOOKS
New York   Toronto   London   Sydney   Auckland

This edition contains the complete text
of the original hardcover edition.
NOT ONE WORD HAS BEEN OMITTED.

NICKAJACK

A Bantam Domain Book / published by arrangement with Doubleday

PUBLISHING HISTORY
Doubleday edition published April 1992
Bantam edition / April 1994

ISBN 0-553-56256-8

Published simultaneously in the United States and Canada

PRINTED IN THE UNITED STATES OF AMERICA

RAD   0 9 8 7 6 5 4 3 2 1

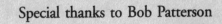

Special thanks to Bob Patterson

Nickajack

Prologue

He did not speak to his wife when he got out of bed that morning. He washed his face and brushed his hair, and he dressed. The woman prepared the breakfast. The children wanted to speak, but over the past year, they had learned that it was no use. He would answer them only if he had to and then usually in monosyllables. He would not look at them, would not touch them. They understood, as much as children can understand such things, for their mother had done her best to explain it to them.

The silence in the small log house was ominous, deathly. It was broken only by the crackling of the fire in the hearth, the bumping and clicking sounds made by the woman as she went mechanically through the motions of preparing the meal, the shuffling of feet on the floor and the occasional nervous coughs and throat-clearings of the children.

The oldest boy then went outside to answer an early morning call of nature, and the noise of the opening and shutting of the door was the greatest intrusion yet into the silence. In a few moments he returned, and he was shivering. As soon as the door slammed behind him, he spoke.

"It's cold outside," he said, but he spoke in the language of the Cherokee people. No response was made. He might as well have spoken to an empty room or to the chill in the outside air, or he might as well have not spoken at all.

The meal was on the table, and they all sat down to eat. They ate in silence, staring most of the time at their own plates, not looking up except when reaching for something, not looking at one another. It was a somber meal.

When they had finished, the man had one last cup of coffee. Then he stood up and buttoned his jacket. He was wearing his best clothes, and the wife thought that he looked rather handsome. She stood up and faced him.

"It's time," he said, speaking Cherokee.

"So soon?" she said.

"Yes. It's time."

Then he turned to the children, and he dropped down on one knee. The children approached him timidly.

"You all know what to do now," he said. "Take care of this place. Take care of your mother. Always look out for each other. Only do what is right and good. I won't be back."

"Not for a long time?" asked the youngest.

"Not ever," said the man. He stood and walked out the door. The woman hesitated, then turned toward the children.

"Stay here," she said, and she followed the man outside. He had walked to a small shed behind the house. The shed was enclosed by a rail fence, and inside the shed a white mule waited indifferently. The man got a braided hackamore from a peg on the wall of the shed and slipped it onto the mule's head. He fastened on the reins, and he tossed a saddle blanket over the animal's back. There was no saddle.

The woman stood shivering in the doorway to the shed. As the man turned to lead the mule out, she spoke.

"The weather will turn bad today," she said. "Perhaps you should wait."

He looked at her and shook his head, then he started toward the door, leading the mule. The woman stepped aside. A fine, cold mist was beginning to fall, and she felt it stinging her face and her hands.

"It's a long ride," she said, "and it will be cold. That jacket won't be enough. I'll get you a blanket."

"No," he said. "You and the children will need the blanket. It won't matter for me."

Suddenly he reached out with his left hand and touched her cheek. The unexpectedness of the movement almost made her flinch.

"I've done everything I can," he said. "The children are good. You'll be all right."

He dropped his hand and turned to mount the mule, but he hesitated. He looked over his shoulder at her. There were no tears. They had passed that stage long ago. She was a strong woman, he thought.

"You're very beautiful," he said, "and you're still young. Find yourself another man."

He was up on the mule and riding away almost before she knew it. She wanted to shout after him. She wanted to stop him. She wanted to plead or to reason, but she only stood there shivering in the icy drizzle and watched him ride away. When he was out of sight, she went back into the house, back to the children.

* * *

The wind was out of the west, and he rode into the wind. Perhaps that was the reason that the cold drops seemed to pelt his face with more ferocity than before. Or perhaps the wind was picking up or the rain increasing in intensity. His fingers grew numb rather quickly, and he felt the damp cold penetrate his body through to the bones. His mind told his body that the cold did not matter, that the pain was of no concern. He rode on.

It must have been about noon, he thought, when the drizzling rain abruptly turned to falling, slashing sheets of ice. The mule, none too fast to begin with, slowed its pace. It hung its head. The man also ducked his head in an attempt to protect his face from the stinging ice. That part of his skin which was exposed, his hands, his face, his ears, all felt frozen. His hair beneath the brim of his hat was stiff with ice. Each breath of frigid air seemed to leave behind a coating of frost on his lungs. He rode on doggedly.

As the ice began to cover the earth with a thin, shiny, translucent coating, the path beneath the mule's hooves became treacherous. Once or twice the beast slipped. It wanted to abandon the fool-hardy journey, turn its backside to the wind and cutting ice, but the man forced it ever forward.

It was late afternoon or early evening. He couldn't be sure because of the storm. The sun had never really shown itself that day. He thought that it was probably early in the evening, because he was coming to the river.

On a good day he would have made the river by late afternoon, crossed at the ford and ridden on into Tahlequah in time for supper. But the vicious ice storm had slowed his pace, had cost him time. He estimated early evening, and he rode on up to the edge of the water. The mule balked. The man could see that the river was up, not too much, but some. It had not yet started to freeze, and it was still moving swiftly. He did not need to touch it to know that it was deathly cold. He urged the mule forward, but the cautious beast stiffened. The man flicked the reins and kicked with his legs, and the mule backed away from the water, resisting stubbornly. The man shouted commands, lashed with the reins and kicked the mule's sides savagely with his heels. Then the mule, in spite of its better judgment, lurched forward, splashing into the icy water, braying out its protest and its fear. The man was caught by surprise and almost lost his seat, but he recovered quickly and shouted and kicked some more.

He felt the river water lap around his legs above his knees, and he thought that his legs had become solid tubes of ice. He continued to kick, but a strange fear entered his head. He thought that his legs might break, snap in two like cold and brittle icicles.

They reached the middle of the river, and the man never knew how or when it happened, but he found himself being swept along by the swift, cold water, and he saw the mule some distance upstream, away from him. The beast had turned around and headed back toward the home side of the river.

The man slapped desperately at the icy water, struggling toward the opposite shore. He had an appointment to keep in Tahlequah. He did not want to die in the icy river. In the midst of his struggles, he experienced a strange phenomenon. He had heard that the entire life of a dying man flashes through his mind.

His did not, but his mind did carry him back a little over a year, and as he flailed at the murderous river, he relived one day.

CHAPTER 1

His name was *Nikutsegi*. It was an old name, even when it had been given to him at birth.

He could remember a time years ago when a white man had asked, "What does it mean?" He had not answered, in fact, had not even understood the question, for he had not known any English at that time. He had later learned to understand and even to speak a little English, but he had never become comfortable with the strange language. They had told him later that the white man had asked for the meaning of his name. And they had answered that it had no meaning. "It's just a name," they had told the white man.

Of course it had a meaning. Or at least it had at one time had a meaning. But even in those days, which now seemed so long ago, there were names of people and of towns and there were other words in the Cherokee language which the people no longer understood. They had lost their meanings. Perhaps they had been part of the old sacred language, most of which had been lost long ages ago when the people had killed the *Ani-Kutani*, the ruling priests, who had become so tyrannical. Whatever the truth of the matter, he had a name that was just a name, and the white men and the breeds who did not speak Cherokee had begun to call him Nickajack, and sometimes even the Cherokees who spoke their language called him that.

Nickajack had never been one to brood. But after he had killed that man, he had not been able to put it out of his mind. He did not know the man's clan, the man known as Common Disturber. But in the old days, the men of Common Disturber's clan would have come for Nickajack. They would have come to kill him, to balance things out between the two clans.

Those ways had changed since the white people had come among them and married into the Cherokee Nation and begun raising mixed-blood families. There were even people among the Cherokees who did not know to which clan they belonged. And since the government of the Cherokee Nation had remodeled itself in the fashion of the United States with a written constitution, there was in effect a new concept of citizenship.

In the old days, if a child had been born of a

Cherokee mother, that is, a woman who belonged to one of the seven clans, then that child was a Cherokee, a member of his mother's clan. However, a child as much as half Cherokee whose Cherokee blood was derived only from his father would not have been considered to be a Cherokee for that child would not belong to a clan. But in the new Cherokee Nation, any child born with a mother or father who had Cherokee blood was called a Cherokee citizen.

Chief John Ross was more white man than Indian, yet his Cherokee blood had come from his mother, and he had been born into a clan. He, at least, was Cherokee according to the old ways. But these younger Ridges and Boudinots and others like them, their fathers had married white women. Their mothers were white. They had no clan, and therefore, according to the old ways, they were not Cherokee. They were, of course, citizens, under the new system. And under the new system, Nickajack had committed a crime against the Cherokee Nation, had broken one of the laws of the land, when he had killed Common Disturber. In the old days that act would have been a crime against Common Disturber's clan.

All of these thoughts troubled the mind of Nickajack as he tried to go about the business of his daily life.

Nickajack was not an intellectual. He had never

been a scholar, and thoughts of this nature were almost painful to his brain. He rose early in the morning, as usual. He wrapped himself in a blanket and walked outside to relieve himself. Back inside the one-room cabin which he had built himself with logs, with the help of his friend and neighbor Coffee Soldier, he added more wood to the fire in the hearth. Then he began to make some coffee. He did that by simply tossing a handful of coffee grounds into a pot of boiling water.

He glanced over at his wife. She was still asleep. His own sleep had been troubled and fitful, and he was up a little earlier than usual. She would wake soon enough, he thought. He went outside again. There were animals to be fed: his white mule, some hogs and chickens. All, he thought, as he went automatically through his chores, all animals brought across the ocean by the white man. His brain felt tired.

And overriding or underneath or behind all of these troubling thoughts was the one big thought, nagging and persistent, the thought that had stimulated all of this unusual brain activity in the head of Nickajack.

He had killed a man.

But that was not really a thought. It was more a feeling or a sort of stunned realization. It was a feeling that he did not like, and it was constant. He would have this uncomfortable feeling, he supposed, for as long as he lived.

There were Cherokees who carried with them through their lives the old honorable "killer" names: *Nunnahi-dihi*, Pathkiller; *Tsata-dihi*, Choctawkiller; *Gusoi-dihi*, Creekkiller; *Yonega-dihi*, Whitekiller; *Nungi-dihi*, Fourkiller; *Sudali-dihi*, Sixkiller; *Sgohi-dihi*, Tenkiller, and others, but that was different. The names were old and had become family names, surnames like the white man used. Originally they had been war titles, and the people who now carried the names had ancestors who had earned them honorably. And the names had been earned by warriors who had killed their enemies.

But Nickajack had killed another Cherokee. If he had earned a name it would be *Tsalagi-dihi*, Cherokeekiller, or perhaps just *Didahihi*, murderer. He did not like the feeling, and he did not like the thoughts which it provoked in his head.

He made himself as busy as he could, tending to the animals, working on a section of fence that really did not need mending, anything to try to keep his mind off the other business. But nothing worked. The tasks were routine manual tasks, leaving his mind free to wander on its own. He was aware of a constant dull pain in his head. He knew that if he could only quit thinking, the ache would go away with the thoughts. But he could not stop. He could not control his own mind.

At lunch he sat with his right elbow on the table, his head resting heavily against the palm of his hand. His wife looked at him, and her brow wrinkled. She knew him well, and she could tell when he was troubled.

"What is it?" she asked.

"My head hurts," he said, but she read his mind. She knew why his head was hurting.

"You had no choice," she said. "There wasn't time to think. You did what any man would have done, and many women, too."

"I killed a man," he said.

"You had no choice."

"He was a Cherokee," said Nickajack, "and I killed him."

When they had finished eating, the children went outside to play. It was cold out. It was the month the Cherokees call *Unoluhtana,* Cold Wind. The white men called it January. And it was a cold January there in the western foothills of the Ozark mountains. Still, the children went outside. When children want to play, they ignore the cold. It doesn't matter to them. Nickajack envied them a little.

He was still sitting at the table there, still holding his head, when the riders came. The children heard them first, but, being children, they did not immediately sound the alarm. They waited and watched until they could see the riders coming, but once they saw them, they ran into the house shouting.

"Someone's coming. Someone's coming."

"A bunch of men on horses."

Nickajack had an old pistol, a .46-caliber Kentucky flintlock converted to percussion. He kept it loaded and hanging on a peg over the fireplace.

He looked up briefly into the eyes of his woman. Her eyes were questioning, pleading. His were desperate. They looked into each other's eyes for only an instant before he stood up and moved across the room to the fireplace.

He reached up and took the pistol from its peg. He checked the load, and then, the pistol in his right hand, he moved to the door.

"Latch the door behind me," he said, and he opened the door and stepped outside. The riders were getting close.

There were six of them, and he could see that they were all well armed. He listened for the sound of the bar falling into place behind him on the other side of the door, and he watched the riders as they came closer and as they began to fan out in a wide semicircle. He stood waiting, the gun in his right hand held down at his side.

The riders moved slowly now, but they did not stop until the one in the middle, directly in front of Nickajack, was close enough for a pistol shot.

"Nickajack," said the rider.

"I am *Nikutsegi,*" he answered. "Who are you?"

"Do you speak English?" asked the rider, for Nickajack had spoken to him in Cherokee.

"Not well," said Nickajack.

The rider looked to his right and called out to another of the men.

"Soap," he said. "Come here."

The man called Soap rode over close to the other one there in front of Nickajack.

"Tell him who we are," said the first man, "and tell him what we're here for."

"My name is *Ohla,*" said Soap, speaking in Cherokee. "This is Captain Scott. We're Lighthorse, from Tahlequah."

Nickajack knew the Lighthorse, *Ani-niyisgi,* the Catchers, Cherokee National Police. He was not quite sure how they could be from Tahlequah. There was hardly anyplace there to be from: the large square laid out for the national capital with its big council shed and two or three small log cabins behind to serve as governmental buildings. Around the square were a few places of business: inns for travelers, the houses of public cooks, and three or four stores.

It was scarcely three years since the John Ross government had arrived from the old homelands over what they were already calling the Trail of Tears or the Trail Where They Cried. The Cherokee speakers usually just called it the Way They Came.

But the John Ross government had selected the spot for the capital of the Cherokee Nation, and they had named it Tahlequah, or *Daligwa*.

Some of the people who did not speak Cherokee were already telling a tale about the name. They said that Chief Ross had sent some men out to look for a place where three streams came together, and there they would build their capital. These men looked and found a nice spot where two streams came together, and then they said, *"Tali eliqua,"* or "Two is enough," and that became the name of the place. But Nickajack knew better than that.

He knew that they simply used an old town name from their original homeland. Back there, in Georgia and North Carolina and the other southern states that had driven the Cherokees west, the white people called that same old word, "Tellico." It was like his name. It was an old word, and its meaning was lost. He stood looking at the Catchers from Tahlequah.

"What do you want?" he asked.

"We've come to arrest you for the murder of Common Disturber," said Soap. "You should put down your gun. We don't want to kill you. There will be a trial."

"That was his name?" said Nickajack.

"Common Disturber," said Soap. "Yes."

"I didn't know him," said Nickajack. "They came at me. Three of them. I defended myself. I didn't even know him. I didn't know any of them. I never killed a man before."

"That's what the trial will be for," said Soap. "You've been charged with the murder of Common Disturber, so we have to arrest you, but at the trial, you can tell your story. If you're not guilty, they'll let you go."

"I killed him," said Nickajack.

"Yes," said Soap, "but the trial will determine whether the killing was murder or self-defense. Put your gun down and come with us."

He could have fired one shot, and maybe he could have killed Soap or Captain Scott, but he had only one shot, and the others would have killed him. Besides, he did not want to kill Soap or the Captain or anyone else. He would not have killed Common Disturber if he had only had time to think or to run. It had all happened before he could think. He had only reacted to the situation. Thinking back, it was as if he had not even really done it. It was as if he had watched someone else.

He leaned slightly to one side and placed the pistol, still uncocked, on a tree stump that stood there beside him.

"*Howa,*" he said. "All right. I'll go with you. Let me get my mule."

And he had ridden into Tahlequah with the Catchers.

CHAPTER 2

Somehow he made it to the other side of the river. For an instant he wondered just how it had happened, for he had no recollection of having gotten himself safely across. He had plunged into the icy water on the back of his mule. Then he had lost his seat. Then apparently his mind had reached back to the day of his arrest, and it had not returned to the present until he had reached the western bank of the river.

He slipped on the ice as he crawled ashore. His hands and feet ached with the cold, and his face felt numb and frozen. He could tell that his wet clothing was already freezing, and when he tried to stand up, he realized that his joints seemed to be frozen, too. His wrists, elbows, knees, all of his normally flexible joints seemed not to want to bend.

Had he been able to stay on the back of the mule, he thought, he would not be in such bad shape. The worst he would have gotten was wet and frozen legs.

But the mule? Where was the mule? He struggled to his feet and turned stiffly from one side to another searching for the truant beast. It was nowhere to be seen. Once more he looked around. The sleet pelted his face, and he thought that perhaps the mule was out there somewhere, and he had simply not seen it. But no. He was alone, and he was freezing.

He had to keep moving or die right there.

He faced west again, and he looked ahead. There before him was a long, gradual, uphill grade. He started to walk, but his knees refused to bend. Each step became an awkward forward jerk of a leg.

How far, he asked himself, must he go? What was it? Three miles? Four? He wasn't sure. He slipped on the ice and fell hard to his knees. It occurred to him that it would be very easy to just stay there and die quietly, but he would not. He must go on. He had an appointment. He managed somehow to get to his feet again, and he continued on his painful and clumsy way up the long hill.

Again he fell, and then he found himself, once more, reliving past events.

*   *   *

He was in the home of Cabin Smith, a full-blood Cherokee, not far from Tahlequah, and he was in chains. The Catchers had brought him there. They had put the shackles on his legs and on his wrists, and they had left him there. Smith's house was small, but it did have three rooms.

Nickajack sat in a straight-backed chair. He was confused. Smith's wife was busy preparing a meal. Smith sat smoking. At last Nickajack spoke in Cherokee.

"Why have they brought me here? Why am I in your home?"

"The Cherokee Nation has no jail." Smith opened his arms with a shrug. "If they arrest someone, they have to use someone's house. I have three rooms, and I'm close to Tahlequah."

"I'm sorry to be the cause of this intrusion," said Nickajack.

"It's all right. They'll pay me. You want some coffee?"

"Yes. Thank you. It was a cold ride."

Smith got up and went to pour some coffee, and he brought a cup to Nickajack. Nickajack took the cup in both of his hands. His hands were still cold from the ride, and the hot cup felt good. He took a tentative sip of the hot, black liquid.

"Wado," he said. "Thank you. It's good."

"We'll have something to eat soon," said Smith.

*   *   *

The Smiths did feed Nickajack. They fed him well, and when Nickajack thanked them for their kindness, Cabin Smith shrugged and said that he would be reimbursed by the Cherokee Nation.

Shortly after that, Colonel Walker appeared on the scene. Nickajack had met Colonel Walker before, but he did not really know the man. He thought that Walker was a friend of Coffee Soldier. Coffee was Nickajack's best friend. They had known each other all their lives. Nickajack did not know whether Colonel Walker was a colonel or not. Perhaps Colonel was his name.

Walker was a robust man, not fat, but stocky, powerfully built. His hair was gray, but that was probably premature. Nickajack could tell by the man's hands that he was a workingman, yet his clothing was expensive. It gave him the look of a rich man. Walker had been to college somewhere. Nickajack knew that, too. At least he had heard that from someone.

He had also heard that Walker had a white grandparent. He noticed that the man's expression was stern. At the door, Walker spoke to Cabin Smith in English.

"Hello, Cabin," he said. "I'm here to see the prisoner."

"Come on in," said Smith. "He's right over there."

Walker stepped across the room to face Nickajack. He studied Nickajack with a stern expression on his face, and that expression did not change, not even when he reached out to shake Nickajack's hand.

"I'm Colonel Walker," he said. "Do you speak English?"

"Not very good," said Nickajack.

"Then we'll talk Cherokee," said Walker, switching to the other language. "Are you all right?"

"Yes," said Nickajack. "I'm all right."

"I'm here to defend you in court," said Walker.

Nickajack gave Walker a curious look but no verbal response.

"I'm your lawyer," said Walker. *"Ditiyohihi."* He used the Cherokee word meaning one who argues.

"Oh," said Nickajack.

"They've charged you with murder," the lawyer continued, "and they claim to have two eyewitnesses. They say that you came upon Common Disturber walking along the road, and you shot him to death. There were two men who saw you fire the shot."

"Yes," said Nickajack. "It's all true. I killed him, and there were two other men there. I didn't know his name, but the Catchers said that it was Common Disturber."

The Colonel rubbed his chin and studied Nickajack's facial expression for a moment.

"You didn't know the man?" he asked.

"No."

"Why did you kill him then?"

"I was going home," said Nickajack. "I had my gun. It's an old gun, but I keep it good. Maybe I shouldn't have carried it. Then I wouldn't have been able to kill that man. I didn't want to kill him. I didn't even know who he was. And he was a Cherokee."

"Why did you kill him?" repeated Walker.

"They came at me," said Nickajack. "They wanted to kill me. I'm not sure why. I think maybe they were at Coffee's house that other time."

"They attacked you first?" said Walker.

"Yes."

"Common Disturber and the other two men? The witnesses?"

"Yes," said Nickajack. "Those three."

"They're lying then," said Walker, and his eyebrows drew a little closer together.

"I did kill him," said Nickajack.

Walker pulled up a straight chair to sit directly in front of Nickajack and look him in the face.

Nickajack looked down at the floor. He knew that white people taught that one should look another in the eyes when conversing, and many Cherokees were adopting the habits of the whites, especially those, like Walker, who had been educated in the white man's schools. He knew, therefore, that Walker did not mean to be rude or impolite or threatening. Still it made him uncomfortable to be stared at like that.

"Nikutsegi," said Walker, still talking in Cherokee, "under the law there are different kinds of killings. There is murder, and there is self-defense. You have been accused of murder, and if they find you guilty, they will hang you. But if those men attacked you, then you killed in self-defense, and if we can prove that in court, then you will go free. Do you understand?"

The question was not meant to be condescending. Walker did not think that Nickajack was stupid, but the written code and the court system were still new to the Cherokees.

The first written law and the first police in the Cherokee Nation dated back only about thirty-three years, to 1808. There had not yet been enough time, Walker knew, for all of the Cherokees to get used to the changes. In the old days—but a generation ago —the killing of a Cherokee by another Cherokee was a matter between clans. It was a matter of balancing things out. If a member of, say, the Wolf Clan killed a member of the Deer Clan, things were seen by the Cherokees as having been thrown out of balance. For balance to be restored, someone from the Wolf Clan, preferably, but not necessarily, the killer, must be killed.

Walker was very much aware that many of the more traditional people had not yet managed the transition from clan system to court system.

"Do you understand?" he said.

"Yes," said Nickajack. "I think so."

Walker was not fully convinced by his client's answer, but he decided to accept it for the time being. There were other things to discuss. It was going to be a tough case, difficult for all the wrong reasons.

"All right," he said. "You know, this is not going to be easy. Not only do they have two lying witnesses, but we're right in the middle of a political battle here. The government is going to want to see you convicted whether you're guilty or not."

"Why?" said Nickajack.

"Because of your politics," said Walker. "They'd like to see all of us dead, all of us in the Ridge Party."

Nickajack started to protest that he was not a member of any political party, but he didn't bother. He was only too aware of the factionalism that had developed in the Cherokee Nation in the past few years.

It had all begun when old Major Ridge, his son John, and his nephews Stand Watie and Buck Watie (Buck had taken the name of Elias Boudinot) suddenly changed their positions on the issue of removal.

Nickajack had never before paid much attention to politics. He'd never really had any interest in it, but the issue of removal had been one that no Cherokee could have ignored.

The states of Georgia, Alabama, North Carolina, and Tennessee had claimed all of the remaining Cherokee lands as their own. They wanted to be rid of the Cherokees once and for all. When Andrew Jackson became President of the United States, the Cherokees at first thought that they would have a powerful ally in this fight, for they had helped Jackson in his war against the Creeks. One Cherokee, since known as Junaluska, had actually saved the general's life on the battlefield at Horseshoe Bend.

But they soon discovered that Jackson's sympathies were not with them, and that the southern states, not the Cherokees, had a new ally in the White House.

They had made this startling discovery in a dramatic way when the very man who had saved Jackson's life had gone to Washington to speak to the new President on behalf of the Cherokees. Jackson had refused to even see the man, and the man had then and there changed his name. *"Tsunuhluhuhski,"* he had said. *He tried and he failed,* and that had become his name, simplified, Anglicized and popularized into Junaluska.

Nickajack could remember that the Cherokees under the newly elected Principal Chief John Ross had for a few years presented a united front of resistance to the Removal Policy. They had taken their case to the United States Supreme Court and had won, but the southern states and the President continued to apply pressure to make them move west. They had lobbied in Washington and worked hard to sway public opinion all up and down the east coast, and they had won a few influential allies among the whites: John Howard Payne, Ralph Waldo Emerson, Henry Clay and David Crockett. But the southern states intensified their efforts against the Cherokees. Georgia had been the worst. The Georgia state government had passed a series of laws which were known as the Anti-Cherokee laws, and they had held a state lottery to give Cherokee lands away to whites.

That was when Major Ridge and his followers had decided that they were fighting a losing battle. They began telling the people to give it up, to move west voluntarily. Two political factions were formed.

The majority of the people remained behind Principal Chief John Ross, who stood firmly against removal. They were called the National Party or the Ross Party. But a number of people followed instead Major Ridge, and they became known as the Ridge Party. Then when Ridge, his son, Boudinot, and eighteen more members of the Ridge Party signed the fraudulent Treaty of New Echota in 1835, they also became known as the Treaty Party.

They signed the treaty agreeing to accept lands in the west in exchange for all their remaining eastern land holdings. They signed the treaty in the name of the Cherokee Nation. They signed it for all Cherokees, even though they had no right. The United States Government had accepted it, even though it had not been signed by any Cherokee Nation officials, had not been authorized by the tribal government. They signed the treaty, and then they moved west.

Nickajack and Coffee Soldier had been there at the signing, although they had not signed the treaty. They had been there among them, and they had actually witnessed the signing, and Nickajack had moved with them because of his friendship for Coffee Soldier.

When the rest of the Cherokees, including Chief Ross, had finally been forced west over the Trail of Tears, their suffering had been great. Four thousand had died, they said. And soon after that, bitter over the suffering and over the loss of their ancient homelands, some members of the Ross Party began to exact justice—or revenge.

In 1839 Major Ridge, John Ridge and Elias Boudinot were all assassinated. And there were other killings, which were answered by retaliatory killings of Ross Party members by members of the Ridge Party.

The factionalism of the Cherokee Nation had almost developed into a full scale civil war. And the killing continued.

Now, according to Colonel Walker, Nickajack had been identified by the Ross Party as a member of the Treaty Party. And the trial which he was about to face was not to be a trial at all, but a political battle, a battle in the war between the two belligerent factions. Major Ridge had been shot from ambush. John Ridge had been pulled from his sickbed and stabbed many times by several different men before the eyes of his horrified wife and small son. Elias Boudinot had been hacked to death on a path in the woods. Now Nickajack was to be tried for murder and if found guilty—as was likely—hanged.

CHAPTER 3

They were inside a small log cabin, one of several on the capital square behind the big shelter. The cabins had been hastily erected to serve as temporary government offices until more substantial facilities could be constructed.

Nickajack and Colonel Walker were seated side by side behind a small table. Off to their right was another table with a man seated behind it, and facing them, a third table and another man. There was an even smaller table off to Nickajack's left almost to the wall. Behind this small table a man sat with his back to the wall facing the wall opposite.

Colonel Walker, speaking Cherokee, told Nickajack that the man to their right was the prosecutor. It would be his job to convince the judge and jury that Nickajack was guilty of murder and should be hanged. The man facing them was the judge. The judge's name was Joseph Spears. The prosecutor's Thomas Lynch. He did not bother to name the other man, except to tell Nickajack that he was the clerk. All of the men except Nickajack and the two Lighthorsemen on either side of the door behind Nickajack were dressed in suits.

"Are these men Cherokees?" asked Nickajack.

"Yes," said Walker. "Of course. This is a Chero-kee court."

"They have white man names."

"Many of us do," said Walker. "They're Cher-okees, but they're Ross men."

"Then they will say that I'm guilty."

"Only a jury can do that," said Walker, "and the prosecutor's job is to convince the jury."

Nickajack looked around the room.

"Who is the jury?" he asked.

"The judge will give us twenty-four names," said Walker. "We can select twelve of them."

Nickajack reflected for a moment.

"If the judge is a Ross man," he said, "then he can give us the names of twenty-four more Ross men from which to pick."

Walker was trying to formulate a response to that remark when the judge cleared his throat and rapped on the table with a small gavel.

"Mr. Lynch," he said, "Mr. Walker, we're ready to begin here. We'll start with a formal reading of the charges. Does your client understand English?"

Walker stood up facing the judge.

"No, Your Honor," he said. "Not well."

"Do you want the court to appoint an interpreter?"

"If it's all right with the court, Your Honor," said Walker, "I can fulfill that role for my client."

"Very well," said the judge. "Nickajack, you've been charged with the willful murder of another human being, a Cherokee citizen by the name of Common Disturber. It is alleged that on the night of November 12 of this year of eighteen hundred and forty, you did meet said Common Disturber on a public road eight miles east of Tahlequah and there did aim and discharge a pistol at said Common Disturber, thereby killing him instantly."

The judge paused while Colonel Walker repeated the charge in Cherokee to Nickajack. Then he continued.

"There were two witnesses to this alleged act of wanton murder who have come forth: to wit, one Hair Campbell and one Thomas Fox Elders."

Again he paused, and again Walker translated for his client.

"You've heard the charges," said Spears. "Now hear the law."

As he read through the following law, he paused now and then to allow Walker to translate.

From the laws of the Cherokee Nation, An Act for the punishment of Criminal Offences. Be it enacted by the National Council, That in all cases of willful murder, the offender, upon trial and conviction by the authorized courts of this Nation, shall suffer death by hanging; and when sentence of death shall have been passed, the courts shall grant a respite of five days before such criminal may be executed; but if the court, with the citizens generally of that section, shall deem it proper, they may petition the Principal Chief to pardon such convicted criminal, who may, if the reasons set forth at large seem to warrant, grant an additional respite for a given number of days, until he can assemble the assistant Chief and Executive Council, who shall duly consider said petitions, with the circumstances and evidence given on trial, and decide by ordering his release and acquittal or execution.

While Walker was translating the last of this, Judge Spears was turning pages. Walker finished, and Spears continued.

Be it further enacted, That . . . if any person shall kill another in self-defense or by accident, without any previous intent to do the same, he shall not be held accountable for such act, and

be exempt from any fine or punishment whatever.

Spears waited for Walker to repeat in Cherokee
this last reading from the law. Then he spoke again.

"Does your client understand the law as I have
read it to him?" he asked.

"Yes, Your Honor," said Walker.

"Very well," said the judge. "I have here a list of
twenty-four names of prospective jurors. It is your
client's privilege as the defendant, with your advice,
to scratch twelve names from this list. The twelve
names remaining will constitute the jury."

The list was handed to Colonel Walker, who took
it to the table and went over the names with Nickajack. Nickajack shrugged and said a word to the
Colonel. The Colonel nodded and looked back toward the judge.

"We would like to question these prospective jurors, Your Honor," he said, "if it please the court."

"That is your privilege, Mr. Walker," said the
judge.

*   *   *

Nickajack lost track of the days. All time seemed to
run together. He lived in the home of Cabin Smith.
He lived in chains. There was almost always an
armed guard at the door, at least one, and maybe

two of the Catchers. Then they were back in the courtroom. In addition to the same ones who had been present before, twenty-four men crowded the small room. Colonel Walker sat with the list of names. He leaned over toward his client and whispered.

"What is your clan?" he said.

"*Ani-sakonige,*" said Nickajack. "The Blue People."

Walker sat up straight and looked up from the paper there before him toward the crowd. He read the first name off the list.

"George Scott," he said. "Would you step forward, please?"

"Step forward, Mr. Scott, and answer any questions Mr. Walker has for you," said Judge Spears.

A man perhaps thirty years old with the appearance of a half-breed stepped over to the table behind which Walker sat.

"You're George Scott?" said Walker.

"Yes."

"Did you know the late Common Disturber?"

"Yes."

"To what clan did he belong?"

"He was a Long Hair."

"What is your clan, Mr. Scott?"

"Long Hair."

"Thank you, Mr. Scott," said Walker. "You're dismissed."

Walker scratched George Scott's name off the top of the list and called the second name. He went through the entire list of twenty-four names asking the same question, and when he had finished, he had eliminated four men, all members of the Long Hair Clan. Then he started over with the names remaining on the list. He called Young Squirrel for the second time.

"Saloli," he said, calling Squirrel by his Cherokee name, "how did you come west?"

"I came with *Guwisguwi,"* said Squirrel, using the Cherokee name of Chief John Ross. "They made us come out here. The soldiers put us in pens like cattle, and they kept us there for a long time. Many got sick, and many died. At last they took us out of the pens, those of us who were still alive, and they made us come out here. Many more got sick and died along the way. I came with *Guwisguwi."*

"And who do you blame for all that suffering?" said Walker.

"The Treaty Party," said Squirrel. "They signed the treaty."

"Saloli," said Walker, "did you know the late Common Disturber?"

"Yes. He was with me on the trail and before that in the pens."

"Do you know the defendant, my client, *Nikut-segi?"*

"I know about him," said Squirrel.

"What do you know about him?"

"He came out here early," said Squirrel, "with the Ridges. He was with them."

"Thank you, *Saloli,*" said Walker.

He scratched the name of Young Squirrel off his list. He called the next name, and Nickajack's mind began to wander away from the business at hand. He had tried to pay attention. After all, they were going to all of this trouble because of him. It was his life they were talking about. But Nickajack felt like he knew already what the outcome was going to be, and besides that, Colonel Walker was shifting from Cherokee to English in the process of interviewing the prospective jurors. The English was hard for Nickajack to pay attention to, and he let his mind wander.

*   *   *

He had been at Coffee Soldier's house that day. He had been there with his whole family, and they had eaten a big meal, the two families together. They had started early that morning, and they had killed and butchered a hog. Coffee Soldier's wife had prepared the meal, and Nickajack's wife had helped.

It had been a good day. The company was good. The children played together. The wives talked together. The two men, two lifelong friends, sat and visited and smoked their pipes.

The conversation had been mostly pleasant, but it had not all been pleasant, for Coffee Soldier had begun talking of politics again and of the unrest in the Cherokee Nation. It had all started, Coffee said, when some of Chief John Ross's followers had killed old Major Ridge and his son John. Then they had killed Elias Boudinot. That's what had started it all. Now there were members of the Ridge Party killing members of the Ross Party in retaliation.

It was like the old clan revenge pattern, only now, he said, it was political parties rather than clans killing each other. He could see no end to it. No one was safe.

"Some of us don't belong to any party," Nickajack had said.

"You have to take sides," said Coffee Soldier. "Anyway you came out here with us. With the Ridges."

"I came out here with you," said Nickajack. "You're my friend."

Nickajack didn't like the turn the conversation had taken. He didn't like the subject of politics. He wasn't at all sure he understood it anyway. He knew he did not like the killings that were taking place within the Cherokee Nation, Cherokees killing Cherokees.

He was almost glad when the conversation was interrupted by the children bursting into the house. They had been playing outside in the cold. Their cheeks and the tips of their noses were bright red, yet they did not rush over to stand by the fire. They ran to their mothers.

"Someone's coming," one of the children said.

"Some men on horses," said another.

Coffee Soldier stood up and walked to the door. Nickajack saw him glance back over his shoulder at the old flintlock rifle hanging above the fireplace. But then he left the rifle there. He opened the door and stepped out onto the porch, leaving the door open behind him.

"Five men coming on horses," he said. "It could be trouble."

Nickajack got up and followed his friend out onto the porch. They stood there side by side watching as the riders came closer. Then a strange thing happened. The riders seemed to pick up speed rather than slow down as they approached the house.

They raced their mounts up to within a few feet of the porch, then jerked back on the reins, stopping abruptly.

"*Kawi Ayosgi,*" said one of the riders, calling Coffee Soldier's name in Cherokee.

"I am he," said Coffee Soldier, also speaking his native language.

"And who is that with you?"

"*Ayuh Nikutsegi,*" said Nickajack, identifying himself.

"I know you," said Coffee Soldier to the man who had spoken. "You are called Archie Drownding."

"Yes," said Drownding. "Then you must know why we're here."

"Who are these other men with you?" asked Coffee Soldier.

"No one here needs to know that," said Archie Drownding. His horse stamped and fidgeted underneath him. Nickajack felt cold, and he noticed that the breath of men and horses alike was coming out in rapid smoke-like puffs.

He thought, *Something bad is going to happen here today,* and then he saw Archie Drownding put his right hand on the hilt of a knife he was wearing in his belt.

"You have no business here," said Coffee Soldier. "No one here signed that treaty. My friend here and his family are just visiting here with us today. We don't mean anything to you."

"But you are one of their party," said Drownding. "You moved with them. You did not come out here with the rest of us. You did not suffer the sickness. You did not bury your own children along the trail."

Nickajack watched with a growing horror as Archie Drownding swung down out of his saddle and pulled the knife from his belt. The other four riders dismounted immediately following Drownding, and things were happening so fast that Nickajack couldn't be sure, but he thought that each of the five men had some sort of weapon in his hand.

He recalled clearly that he saw two hatchets.

"I'll get my gun," said Coffee Soldier in a hurried and harsh whisper, and he faded back into the house. Nickajack moved to block the doorway, instinctively protecting his friend and their families inside the house. The five men moved menacingly toward him.

"Stay back," said Nickajack.

The men kept moving, getting closer. The weapons were raised.

"Our women and children are inside," said Nickajack. "Go back."

"We buried women and children all along the trail," said Drownding.

Two men moved quickly, suddenly up on the porch, one on either side of Nickajack, and he felt them grab his two arms and pull. He struggled, but he was helpless, stretched out there before the raised knife of Archie Drownding.

He saw the knife poised for an instant above his head, and then he heard the deafening roar in his ears as Coffee Soldier fired the rifle behind him. A black hole appeared in Archie Drownding's chest, and the man's expression turned first to surprise, then pain. He watched as the fingers relaxed and the knife fell to the porch and the lifeless body toppled back to sprawl half on the porch, half on the frozen ground beyond.

There were shouts, and the men holding Nickajack's arms released him and ran to pick up the body of their fallen comrade. In a moment it was over, and they were gone.

CHAPTER 4

There had been no immediate reprisals. A week had passed, then another. Nickajack and Coffee Soldier had met and talked it over.

"They probably didn't even report it," said Coffee. "They attacked us at my home. If they told it, they would be the ones arrested. They could try to lie about how it happened, but there are four of them, and there are all of us—four adults and all of our children. It would be their story against our story."

"So nothing will come of it?" said Nickajack.

"They won't report us to the Catchers," said Coffee Soldier, "but they won't forget us either."

So life went on for Nickajack more or less as usual, but he did start to carry his old pistol when he ventured out away from his house. And it was as if a black pall had been cast over the lives of Nickajack and Coffee Soldier and both of their families. The children still played, as children will no matter what happens around them, but the conversations between the two friends and between husband and wife in both households became shorter and more somber. Lovemaking became less frequent and more perfunctory. Facial expressions grew long and dark and almost painful.

They had known of the violence before. They had been aware of the bitter factionalism which divided their people. But now they were experiencing it personally, firsthand, at close range. Coffee Soldier had shot a man, another Cherokee, right before the eyes of Nickajack, and almost certainly, if he had not, Coffee and Nickajack would both have been killed, and there was no telling what might have happened to their families. And their lives were threatened still. Nickajack began to carry a dark sense of foreboding with him wherever he went.

And always there were more stories about the violence raging around the Cherokee Nation. Almost all of the actual signers of the Treaty of New Echota were dead at the hands of the avengers from the Ross Party, and friends or political allies of the Ridges actively sought revenge.

The most notorious of these were the Starrs. James Starr had moved west with the Old Settlers. They had moved early, before the Treaty Party, even before the treaty had been signed. The Old Settlers had established their own government, which had become known as the Cherokee Nation West, and they wanted to keep that government. The Treaty Party, upon arriving in the west, had expressed its willingness to live under the government of the Old Settlers. The Ross Party, however, insisted that the John Ross administration was the only legitimate Cherokee Nation government.

As a result, the Treaty Party found themselves a new set of allies in the Cherokee Nation West. Even so, they were still greatly outnumbered by the Ross Party. Any unification of the three factions of Cherokees leading to an eventual election would assure that John Ross would remain Chief.

James Starr's sons, Tom, Bean and Ellis, and a handful of their friends had begun seriously harassing the supporters of John Ross. They had killed. They had burned homes. They had disrupted public meetings and elections. Then some members of the Ross Party had gone to the home of James Starr. They had killed James and a younger brother of Tom, Bean and Ellis. The fury of the Starrs intensified.

Nickajack heard tales about all of this and more, and it troubled his ordinarily calm spirit. His visits to his friend Coffee Soldier became less frequent, for the talk always seemed to turn to politics and to the violence. Nickajack did not want to dwell on these subjects, and it was difficult enough for him to keep them off his mind when he was alone or with his own family.

He decided that he did not need Coffee Soldier around bringing up the subject in conversation. Nickajack had known that the move west would constitute a major disruption of his life, but he had made the decision to move anyway. He had not been prepared for the nature or the intensity of that disruption. He tried to stay at home as much as possible, but now and then, he had to venture out, and, of course, when he did, he carried his gun.

*   *   *

It was midafternoon, and it was cold, but it was not bitter cold. Nickajack, riding his white mule, was wearing his big coat, and underneath it, his pistol was tucked into the waistband of his trousers. There was money in his pocket, for he had just come from Eli Johnson's store only a few miles from his home. He had taken Johnson some furs, and Johnson had bought them all. Nickajack was well pleased with the transaction. He was riding along at a slow but steady pace, and then he saw, up ahead in the road, three men standing facing him. As he rode closer, it seemed to him that the three were just watching him, waiting for him.

They were all Indians. He could tell that. Fullbloods, or close to it. As he rode closer yet, he thought that he could recognize two of the men, the two shorter ones. He was almost sure that they had been among the five who attacked him and Coffee Soldier at Coffee's house.

The third man, the one who stood in the middle, he did not know. That one stood leaning on a long rifle. The one to his right held a club in his hand. The man to his left stood with his hands on his hips, but Nickajack could see an ax hanging in the man's belt.

He reined in the mule and waited, but the three men did not move. It seemed obvious then to Nickajack that they were waiting for him. And they were blocking the road. Nickajack felt his heart beat faster, as he urged the mule forward—slowly.

Still the men did not move. He rode to within twenty feet of them and stopped again.

"'*Siyo*," he said, greeting them in Cherokee. They stared at him but did not respond. After a tense pause, the man with the club spoke to the man with the long rifle.

"He was there," he said, speaking Cherokee. "He's one of those who killed Archie Drownding."

Nickajack considered arguing with the men, protesting his innocence, but he did not. He decided against it. It would have been futile, for he could tell that their minds were made up.

"You're blocking my way," he said. "Let me pass."

Even as he spoke, he wondered just what he might do if the men actually stepped aside to let him pass. In order to ride on, he would have to turn his back to them.

He looked at them carefully. The short one with the club was stocky and dressed in ragged homespun clothing. The one in the middle with the rifle who seemed to be the leader still stood resting a forearm on the muzzle of the long barrel. He was well dressed in what Nickajack took to be store-bought clothes. He wore black shiny boots and had a colorful blanket thrown over his shoulders. His hair was long, and he had a thin mustache which grew down past the corners of his mouth. The third man was thin and scruffy.

All three wore menacing expressions on hard faces, and they stared, rudely, threateningly at Nickajack. At last the one in the middle spoke.

"What is your name?" he asked.

"Ayuh Nikutsegi," said Nickajack. "And yours?"

The man slowly raised his rifle. Nickajack quickly reached under his coat and pulled out the pistol, cocking it, pointing and firing. The lead ball hit the rifleman in the middle of the forehead, splattering blood.

The man's head jerked backward once, then bobbed back and forth foolishly on his shoulders as he began falling back. As he fell, his finger jerked the trigger of his rifle, sending its ball harmlessly into the air. The body had not yet hit the ground when Nickajack kicked the sides of his mule and raced straight ahead.

The other two men shouted and jumped to the sides of the road. As Nickajack rode away from them, they flung their weapons after him, but both fell far short of the mark, and Nickajack was safely away.

*   *   *

He sat across the table from his wife. She could tell that something was wrong. She poured him a fresh cup of coffee and set it on the table there before him and waited. He stared at the tabletop in deadly silence.

"What is it?" she said.

"I have just killed a man," he said. "Just now."

"Who was he?" she said.

"A Cherokee," he said. "I never saw him before."

"Then why? How did it happen?"

Nickajack sipped at the hot coffee. It tasted good, and it felt good as it warmed his insides, but it did not help to calm his ragged nerves. He put the cup down.

"There were three men," he said. "They stood across the road in my path. I recognized two of them from that day at Coffee's house. The other one was a stranger to me. He had a rifle, and he raised his rifle as if to shoot at me. I shot him first, and I rode away. That's all."

"Will they say anything, do you think?"

"I don't know," said Nickajack. "This time was different from the other. I don't know."

Later they had their supper, and they went through the rest of the day as if nothing unusual had happened. They went through the day as usual except that they hardly spoke. They moved about like ants doing their chores, and when the sun went down and the sky grew dark, they went to bed, and they lay on their backs and stared at the darkness of the ceiling over their heads. Sometime far into the night they drifted into uneasy sleep, and it was after lunch the next day when the Catchers came for him.

CHAPTER 5

He was back in the courtroom. To his right sat
Colonel Walker. The prosecutor, Lynch, was at his
table farther to the right, and the judge and clerk
were in their usual positions. The two Catchers were
at the door. This day, however, there were more
people in the courtroom. Against the far wall to
Nickajack's right, the twelve-man jury was seated,
and behind Nickajack the small gallery was packed
with curious spectators. The day had turned a little
colder, and a fire tender had been added to the
courtroom staff. Nickajack had lost all track of time.
He did not know how many days and nights he had
spent in the home of Cabin Smith, and he did not
know how many days he had spent in the courtroom. For all he knew, he might have been in the
courtroom for several days and nights straight.

His mind kept taking him back in time, so that

his lucid moments in the present were confused. There was no past, no present, no future. It was all the same in his mind.

"Gentlemen of the jury," Lynch intoned, "a fellow tribesman, a citizen, a neighbor has been brutally and wantonly murdered on a public road. Our nation is at present entangled in a web of violence, and the present case is but one instance of the many. It has to be stopped. It has to be stopped for our wives and children to be safe once again. It has to be stopped in order for us to get on with the serious business of rebuilding our nation out here in the west.

"Unfortunately we have not been able to apprehend the perpetrators of these violent deeds in most cases, and we are in grave danger of seeing a return of the old blood revenge pattern of our ancestors. But here and now we have a chance to show our citizens and to show the United States that we do live by laws, that in the Cherokee Nation justice will be done.

"Gentlemen of the jury, we have two witnesses who have come forth voluntarily to testify in this trial, two witnesses to the senseless killing of our friend and neighbor Common Disturber. With the help of these two brave and honest citizens, I intend to prove to you that the defendant in this trial, the man known by the name of Nickajack, seated just there in this courtroom, is guilty of that murder and is deserving of the severest penalty under our laws—death by hanging."

Nickajack recalled the killing of Archie Drownding and the fact that nothing had come of it, that Drownding's accomplices obviously had not reported the incident to anyone for fear of incriminating themselves. He recalled that he had wondered if the same thing would be true in this present case. Well, he had certainly been wrong about that.

Not only had the two reported the killing of Common Disturber, they were to appear as witnesses against Nickajack, and it was obvious that their intent was to lie about the circumstances of the killing.

Colonel Walker was right, too, thought Nickajack. *This is not going to be a real trial. It will be a battle between political factions. And I am to be the prize.*

He knew, too, or at least he thought that he knew, what the outcome would be. The judge, the prosecutor, the jury, and the two witnesses were all on the same side. Their only opposition was Colonel Walker. And then there was the truth, and the truth was that Nickajack had killed a man, a Cherokee.

He recalled the killing in vivid detail, and it made him feel sick inside. He was sick for what he had done, and he was sick for what it had done to his life and the lives of his wife and children. But then it occurred to him that it was not just the killing of

Common Disturber that had brought him to the courtroom. No. Other things had led to it.

It was as if major forces had been long at work with the object of bringing him to this end. It was the killing of Archie Drownding that had brought about the killing of Common Disturber. But even that was not the beginning. Archie Drownding and the others had gone to Coffee Soldier's house for a reason. They had gone there to kill Coffee and maybe to kill Nickajack because Coffee and Nickajack were associated with the Ridges, with the treaty signers. Were the treaty signers then the ones to blame? Other events had caused them to sign.

Someone was talking in the courtroom, but Nickajack wasn't listening. His mind traveled back to his former home in the east.

Nickajack could not remember a time when the Cherokees had not had trouble with the whites. There had been no war in his lifetime with the whites, but it seemed, thinking back over the years, that there had been almost constant pressure from the whites for Cherokee land. Once the Cherokees had owned or controlled a vast domain that covered all or parts of the states of North Carolina, South Carolina, Kentucky, Tennessee, Georgia, Alabama and West Virginia.

By the time of Nickajack's earliest remembrance, those landholdings had been chopped down considerably by treaties. There were always new treaties, in spite of the fact that each treaty had been written as if it were to be the final one and would be in effect forever.

The Cherokees' first treaty had been signed with Englishmen from the colony of South Carolina in 1721. From that time until the dreadful Treaty of New Echota, the fraudulent removal treaty, they had signed a total of thirty-eight treaties, thirty-eight solemn pledges of perpetual peace and friendship, thirty-eight promises that no more land would be demanded, that Cherokee ownership to remaining lands would be honored and respected.

But Nickajack could remember from his early childhood, from before he was even ten years old, listening to the adults talking about the United States Government and its attempts to get all the Cherokees to move west. It seemed as if the white people of Georgia and North Carolina and South Carolina and Alabama did not want Cherokees for neighbors. And a good many Cherokees did move west. They gave into the pressure from the United States, or they just got tired of being annoyed, but they moved west. These were the ones who would become known as the Old Settlers.

Then when Nickajack had been about seventeen years old, things started happening quickly. The pressures increased. It had become next to impossible to even keep up with the news.

In 1828 the Cherokees in the west signed a new

treaty with the United States. This treaty gave the Cherokees large western landholdings. Of course, looking back, one could see that what the treaty really accomplished was to provide the United States with a place to send the unwanted Cherokees to get them out of the way.

Just the year before, the Cherokees still in the east, in the homeland, had drafted a new Cherokee Constitution and established the Cherokee Nation as a republic with Chief John Ross in the presidency. The Georgians claimed that the Cherokees had violated the United States Constitution by establishing a state within a state, and a war of words erupted between Georgia newspapers and the Cherokee tribal newspaper, *The Cherokee Phoenix*. Then gold was discovered in Georgia Cherokee country.

White gold seekers had flooded onto the Cherokee lands, and the state of Georgia gave them its blessing, claiming the land for its own. It also maintained that state laws extended over Cherokees living on those lands. It declared Cherokee laws and customs to be null and void, and the Cherokees living on those lands abandoned their homes to the greedy hordes and fled to other parts of the Cherokee Nation.

In 1830 the United States Congress passed what it called the Indian Removal Act. The new law provided for an exchange of western lands for lands held by Indians in the east, and the state of Georgia responded by passing its own series of anti-Cherokee laws. They forbade the Cherokee courts or council to meet except to ratify land cessions, forbade them to mine their own gold, authorized a survey of Cherokee land in order to distribute it to Georgians by state lottery, made it illegal for white missionaries to live among the Cherokees, and created the Georgia State Guard to terrorize the Cherokees in their own homes.

Nickajack could remember those days. He could remember friends of his who had been beaten by the Georgia Guard. He had heard of women having been raped by them, and he had actually seen houses that the Guard had burned to the ground, leaving Cherokee families homeless. When people resisted the Georgia Guard, they were arrested and thrown into prison.

Even the Reverend Worcester had been thrown into prison by the Georgia Guard. Nickajack had not known Reverend Worcester, but he had heard about him. Worcester had been living among the Cherokees for some time, and everyone knew of him. When Sequoyah had given the Cherokees the writing system, the way to write their own language, Worcester had worked with him to get type cast so that they could begin publishing the *Phoenix* in both Cherokee and English, and Worcester had been working with Elias Boudinot on a Cherokee language translation of the New Testament. But the

Georgia Guard had arrested Worcester for living on Cherokee land and for refusing to swear to an oath of allegiance to the state of Georgia.

Nickajack recalled how the news of Worcester's arrest had astonished him. He remembered that Worcester's case had gone all the way to the United States Supreme Court, and Worcester had won. The Cherokees had won. And there had been much celebrating in the Cherokee Nation when the news had arrived. But hard on its heels came more news.

When informed of the Supreme Court decision, President Andrew Jackson had said, "John Marshall has made his decision; now let him enforce it."

Nickajack recalled hearing that news, too, and he remembered that when he heard it, he had wondered where John Ross, Major Ridge, John Ridge and Elias Boudinot were just at that time. They were the ones on whom all the Cherokees' hopes rested. They were the leaders. They were the ones who knew how to deal with the white man, knew his laws and his lawmakers. Nickajack had thought that they were probably in Washington City right at that moment talking to Congressmen. He had faith that they would set things right.

No one could make the Cherokees leave their own country, not Georgia, not the United States. He would wait. All the Cherokees would wait until these tribal leaders told them what to do.

CHAPTER 6

Coffee Soldier had come to Nickajack's house. He was out of breath from running, and when he finally stopped panting, Nickajack gave him food and coffee. He ate hurriedly, for he had brought news, and he was anxious to talk.

"I've just come from the Council at Red Clay. The delegates have all just returned from Washington. People were there from all of the Cherokee towns, from all over the Cherokee Nation. You should have gone with me."

"I had work to do here," said Nickajack. "What happened at the Council?"

"John Ross talked first. He said that our lands were given to us by God, and that they are meant to be ours forever. He said that even the United States Supreme Court has admitted that this is our land, and that we are a nation, and that our land cannot be taken away from us. He said that he knows how difficult it has been. The Georgians have already had their lottery, and some white men went to John Ross's own home and threw him out with his wife and children. They are now living in a small cabin across the Tennessee line, there near Red Clay."

"They took our Chief's house?" said Nickajack.

"Even so," said Coffee.

"Then no one is safe."

"Still he says that we should hold on. It's our land. Georgia is acting illegally."

"But if someone takes our house away from us and our fields, then where should we go?"

"Go build another house or live with a friend or relative," said Coffee. "They are just trying to pressure us into signing away our lands with another treaty. We should not give in. That's what John Ross said."

There was a long pause, and Nickajack got up to refill their coffee cups. He sat back down with a troubled expression on his face.

"John Ridge was there, too," said Coffee, "with his father and Elias Boudinot. John Ridge spoke to us in Cherokee. He said that everything the Chief said was true. He said that he had fought long and hard and supported our Chief in his efforts. He said that, like the rest of us, he thought that we had won when the Court said that we were right. But then he said that his hopes were dashed when the President refused to follow the ruling of the Court. He no longer has any hope, he said."

Coffee paused to sip from his cup and to let that news soak in. Nickajack's brow wrinkled in thought.

"He said that the Georgians have been encouraged by the President's reaction to the Court, and they are overrunning our country," Coffee continued. " 'We are not safe in our own homes. Look at what has happened to even our Chief,' he said. Then he said, 'I think the state of Georgia is committing a crime against our nation. I think the United States is committing a crime against our nation.' And then he said, 'But I have come to believe that the greatest crime is to continue to hold out false hopes for our people, to convince them to stay here and suffer and die when we now know that the outcome is inevitable.' That's what he said."

"But what does it all mean?" said Nickajack.

"Elias Boudinot said the rest of it," Coffee answered. "He said that no matter what we do, the United States Government is going to make us move to the west. If we continue to resist, they'll make it that much harder on all of us. So he said we should sign a new treaty and move. That way, at least, the move will be easier for us, and the Georgia Guard will leave us alone until we can get out."

"What do you think?" said Nickajack.

"I believe what John Ross says when he says that we are right and they are wrong," said Coffee. "I believe that. But what the Ridges are now saying makes sense to me, too."

*   *   *

Nickajack had walked out into the woods that evening. He walked in his bare feet and felt the earth beneath him. He heard the birds singing, and he knew them all by their songs. There was *tsisquaya*, the little sparrow, the real bird; there was *dojuwha*, the red bird, the bright cardinal; there was *tlutlu*, the martin; *dalala*, the red-headed woodpecker; *tsayoga*, the loud, scolding blue jay; *tsitsi*, the little wren. Would these same birds be in the west, he wondered. He had no idea what was in the west. Up over his head in the branches of a large tree, *saloli*, the squirrel, chattered. He looked up, and there he saw *galegi*, the blacksnake, slithering along one of the lower branches.

He stopped and put his hands on the large, solid trunk of an oak tree, *adayahi*, and he thought that he could feel the sap coursing through its veins. He knew the trees, too, all of them: *wanei*, the hickory, *tsuhwagi*, the maple, *kaloquegidi*, the locust, *atisuhgi*, the birch, *gusuh*, the beech, *tsuganonuh*, the ash, *dawajila*, the elm. He knew them all.

He stepped away from the tree and resumed his walk, feeling the earth, the dirt, the rocks, the grass, listening to the sounds around him, the sounds of the woods, of the land that was his home, the land that he knew so intimately. And yet, in a strange way, it was almost as if he were walking through these woods for the first time, seeing the sights for the first time, hearing the old familiar sounds for the first time. He came to the edge of the swift mountain stream, and he sat down, putting his feet into the cold water.

"*Ama,*" he said, "Water, I know you, too, and I know all of your creatures."

Down below among the rocks was *tsisduh,* the crawdad. The waters were alive with fish: *unanuhtsaduh atsadi,* the speckled trout, *tsuloluhdi atsadi,* the rainbow trout, *oliga,* the fish called red horse, and *daloge,* hog sucker. And more. Many more, and he knew them all. There was *duhdegi,* the eel, *doyi,* the beaver, and *gawanuh,* the duck, all creatures of the water. Nickajack knew them all, and he called them all by name.

He knew where *doyi* built his dams and where the eagle, *uwohali,* nested. He knew *awi,* the deer, and *yona,* the bear. He knew *tsula,* the fox, *walosi,* the frog, and *waya,* the wolf. He knew where to look for grapes and onions and mushrooms and all of the wild greens. He knew the names of the rivers and streams, the mountains and the valleys, and he was afraid that he would be a stranger in the west. He would not know the names of places and things, and they would not know him.

He wondered what the west was like. He wondered if he would wind up living in the west. According to Coffee, the Ridges had said that the move was inevitable.

Up in the sky, a cloud moved out from in front of the sun, and sunlight suddenly gleamed off the surface of a small, round rock just in the water there beside Nickajack. The gleam caught his eye, and he reached for the rock. It was wet and cold and smooth, and he held it in his hand. His fingers closed over the rock, the small piece of his homeland, and he stood up to walk back to his house. Along the way, he dropped the rock into a pocket of his trousers.

*   *   *

It was a month or so later when Coffee came again. There was to be another Council at Red Clay. Everyone should be there, he said. Nickajack decided that he would attend this one, and the two men made plans to travel together to Red Clay.

*   *   *

He had never seen so many people in one place. He heard all of the three dialects of the Cherokee language being spoken there, and he heard English. He saw people in buckskin leggings and hunting shirts and turbans, and he saw people dressed in the style of the white man. He saw full-blood Indians and mixed-bloods and some who had the appearance of white people. And he discovered that there were even a few white people there.

There was a shelter for the meeting, like an arbor but much bigger, a roof over tall, stout poles. The space underneath the arbor was mostly filled with rough benches, but at one end of the space there was a long table with chairs behind it and a podium placed on top in the middle.

The meeting had been delayed because John Ross had not yet made his appearance. It was raining, and the speculation was that the rains had likely delayed the Chief's travel. Out around the council shed, the people had pitched tents or constructed temporary brush shelters and small arbors. Nickajack and Coffee found some friends under an arbor and joined them there. They had a fire and were cooking.

They spent that night on the damp ground underneath the arbor, but they had been well fed.

The following morning John Ross showed up, and the people gathered underneath the council shed until there was no more room. Then more gathered around it on all four sides. For such a large crowd, they were amazingly quiet. Everyone wanted to hear everything that was said. Nickajack leaned close to Coffee Soldier.

"Is that our Council behind the long table?" he asked.

"Yes," said Coffee. "It's called the National Committee."

One man stood up and moved to the podium. He was a short man, conspicuously so. He was well dressed, in the manner of a wealthy plantation owner, and he was not recognizably Indian.

"Is that *Guwisguwi?*" said Nickajack, using Ross's Cherokee name.

"Yes," said Coffee.

"I thought so," said Nickajack. He knew that Chief Ross was more Scottish by blood than he was Cherokee, and he knew that some Cherokees called the Chief by the nickname *Tsan Usdi,* meaning Little John. Ross laid some papers out on the podium and cleared his throat in preparation to speak.

Nickajack decided to keep quiet and listen.

"Friends and fellow citizens," said Ross, his voice strong and clear, "you have once more met in your legislative capacity for the purpose of deliberating upon the affairs of this nation, and to adopt such measures as its interest and welfare shall seem to demand. Therefore, as a preliminary step, I will take a cursory view of such topics as in my opinion commands your attention."

Ross paused to allow a translator to render his words into Cherokee for those in the crowd who did not understand English. He then reviewed the history of the relationship between the Cherokee Nation and the United States, leading up to the United

States Congress's recent passing of the Removal Act. He explained to the people his belief that the real purpose of the United States Government was to combine all the Indian tribes into one Territory and then to make them "an integral part of the United States."

There was more at stake than just a move, he insisted. The very existence of the Cherokee Nation as a separate and sovereign nation was threatened. Nickajack tried hard to comprehend all this, and he listened carefully as Ross concluded his speech.

"In the present state of things, you can do little more by legislation than to adopt such measures as will be calculated to keep our citizens correctly informed of the true posture of the public affairs, that they may remain united in the support of our common interests and national rights, also securing the administration of justice between individuals in their private transactions so far as it may be practicable to do so. Confiding in the justice of our cause and the righteous decision of the Supreme Court of the United States upon it, and also in the constitutional power of the Federal Government to have it executed, we cannot but hope that the virtue of the people of the United States will ultimately control the faithful execution of their treaty obligations for our national protection, and under this reliance, let us still patiently endure our oppressions and place our trust under the guidance of a Benignant Providence."

As John Ross moved to take his seat, the crowd of gathered Cherokees gave him thunderous applause and loud, enthusiastic cheers. It was obvious to Nickajack that the vast majority of those present stood firmly behind their Chief.

When they finally quieted down, a white man, a representative of the United States Government, spoke. He read a letter from Lewis Cass, the Secretary of War, and presented the Cherokees with a proposal from the United States, a proposal to exchange their land for lands in the west.

The Cherokee Council voted to reject the proposal.

Then John Ridge spoke. He begged the people to listen to reason. He warned them that the longer they attempted to hold out against the Federal Government the more intense their suffering would become. The Council at last voted to send a delegation to Washington, headed by Chief Ross.

Nickajack was puzzled. The meeting was over, and, as far as he could determine, nothing had been accomplished. People still hung around the council grounds in clusters, talking among themselves about what had happened there, or about what had not happened.

Coffee Soldier joined a group that had gathered around John Ridge, and Nickajack followed him, hanging back some small distance and waiting. He noticed that people in other groups were looking in their direction, and the looks on their faces were hard. It appeared to Nickajack that the Cherokee people were dividing themselves up into two camps, each one hostile toward the other.

He was quiet when Coffee finally broke away from the others to rejoin him. He was quiet as they began their journey back toward home. When at last he spoke to Coffee, it was brief, direct, matter of fact.

"There's going to be trouble," he said.

CHAPTER 7

Thomas Fox Elders had sworn to tell the truth, but Nickajack knew that the man was lying. He was seated in a chair beside the judge's table, and the prosecutor, Mr. Lynch, was asking him questions.

"Mr. Elders," Lynch was saying, "just tell us what you saw that day. In your own words."

Elders spoke in English.

"Me and Hair," he said, "we was just walking across the field."

"You're speaking of Hair Campbell?" said Lynch.

"Yeah. Me and Hair was walking across the field, and we saw Common Disturber walking along the road. We thought that we'd catch up to him and talk to him. He was a friend of ours."

"Had the late Common Disturber seen you?" asked Lynch.

"No," said Elders. "He didn't see us. He was just

walking along, minding his own business, so we thought that we'd go catch up with him and talk to him, but then we seen this man come riding along toward Common Disturber, coming from the other way, you know."

"Is this man in this courtroom?" said Lynch.

"Yes, sir, he sure enough is. He's that one right over there."

Elders pointed.

"Indicating the defendant, Mr. Nickajack," said Lynch. "Go on, Mr. Elders. What happened?"

"Well, this Nickajack, he came along riding on a mule, a white mule, and he saw Common Disturber there in the road in front of him. He stopped his mule, and they talked a little, I guess. We wasn't close enough to hear."

"Nickajack and Common Disturber talked together?"

"Yeah. I guess they did. That's what it looked like. Me and Hair, we just kept walking that way, but then all of a sudden like, this Nickajack, he pulled a pistol out from under his coat, and he shot Common Disturber. Then he rode off."

"Was there no provocation?"

"Huh?"

"Did it look to you as if Common Disturber did or said anything to provoke Nickajack into the shooting?"

"Oh," said Elders. "He might've said something.

I don't know. I wasn't close enough to hear. But I sure didn't see him do nothing. He was just standing there in the road."

"Thank you, Mr. Elders." Lynch turned to walk back to his seat. "Your witness, Mr. Walker," he added over his shoulder.

Walker sat for a moment and stared at Elders. Then he stood up and walked over to stand beside the witness's chair. He rubbed his chin, and he cleared his throat.

"Mr. Elders," he said, "is it not true that you and Mr. Campbell were in the road with Common Disturber together when my client came riding up?"

"No, sir. We was walking across the field."

"Is it not true that the three of you, armed, were waiting in the road, blocking the path of Nickajack as he made his way home?"

"No," said Elders. "That ain't true."

"Is it not true that Common Disturber was armed with a long-barreled rifle gun, the which he meant to use on my client, Nickajack?"

"I didn't see no rifle gun."

"Is it not true that my client only pulled out his pistol and fired at Common Disturber in self-defense after Common Disturber raised his rifle gun to fire at my client?"

"No, sir," said Elders. "That ain't what happened. I didn't see no rifle gun."

Walker turned and paced away from Elders a few steps. Then he turned back to face him again.

"Mr. Elders, had you ever seen my client before the day on which Common Disturber was shot and killed?"

"I don't believe that I ever seen him before in my life."

"Did you and Mr. Campbell in the company of Mr. Archie Drownding and two other men ride to the home of one Coffee Soldier with the intent of killing Mr. Soldier, and wasn't Nickajack present on that day?"

"No, sir."

"And wasn't Mr. Drownding himself killed there?"

"I heard that something happened to Archie," said Elders, "but I didn't really know. If that's what happened, I didn't know nothing about it. I wasn't there. I don't know no one named Soldier."

"Mr. Elders," said Walker, "what is your clan?"

"I'm a Wolf."

"What is your political affiliation?"

"I don't know what that means."

"Do you consider yourself to be a member of the National Party led by Principal Chief John Ross?"

"I don't know anything about that," said Elders. "I think that Chief Ross is doing the right things."

"How did you come to this country, Mr. Elders?" asked Walker.

Elders's jaws clenched and his brows drew together. His eyes narrowed to slits.

"I .walked," he said. "Every step, I walked. And
soldiers at my back the whole time. And me cough-
ing. Spitting blood. I buried my wife and my baby. I
barely had time to pray over their graves, and if I
was to go back looking, I bet I couldn't even find
them today. I walked, and I'm lucky I made it
alive."

"No further questions, Mr. Elders." Walker resumed his seat beside Nickajack.

Mr. Lynch called Hair Campbell to the witness
stand. Campbell was sworn in, and Lynch began to
question him. He told the same story as had Elders.

Somewhere along the line, Nickajack had ceased
to listen. His mind had carried him back again to
the old country, to a time that in some ways seemed
a lifetime ago, in others it seemed as near, as present
as the courtroom in which he sat.

*   *   *

They had gathered at New Echota. The Ridges and
Boudinot were there, and there were white men
there who represented the United States Government. Nickajack had expected great crowds of people, the way it had been at Red Clay, but it was a
small gathering there at New Echota, perhaps three
hundred and fifty people. Many of them, Nickajack

noticed, were mixed-bloods. There were few full-bloods. Apparently there were no followers of Chief John Ross. It was Saturday, December 19, 1835.

Nickajack knew a few of the people there, and he spent time talking to them. Coffee knew many of them, and he introduced Nickajack around.

The talk was that a treaty would be signed at this meeting. Nickajack was surprised to hear that. There was also talk that John Ross had sent out the word to all of his followers to stay away, and that was why there were so few people there. Nickajack was pretty sure that the followers of the Chief far outnumbered those of the Ridges, and he wondered why, if Ross was opposed to the treaty, he would not want his people there to vote it down. But then he realized that without Ross and his Council, the treaty would not be legal.

This gathering was nothing more than just that, a great gathering of like-minded people. How could they sign a treaty without the official representatives of the Cherokee Nation? The talk confused him.

Two more days passed in idle conversation and waiting. It was rumored that one of the important white men was at home ill, and that they were waiting for him to recuperate and arrive on the scene. On the morning of Tuesday, December 22, the meeting finally got underway. They gathered underneath a council shed, much like the one at Red Clay.

Nickajack heard the names of the presiding officer, John Gunter, and the Secretary, Alexander McCoy. Both were mixed-bloods. Both had the appearance, to Nickajack, of white men. The main negotiator for the United States was a man named Schermerhorn. Nickajack had heard of him. He was a preacher, but the followers of Chief Ross, those who opposed the treaty, called him Devil's Horn.

Most of that day, Devil's Horn talked. He talked about how difficult things were getting to be for the Cherokees, and he told them how, if they moved west, they would leave all those difficulties behind them. There would be no white people pressing upon their lands. There would be no more government demands for more treaties and land cessions. Game would be abundant. Devil's Horn also told the crowd gathered there that the United States Government looked upon this meeting as a legal Council of the Cherokee Nation and the Government would assume that any Cherokees not present at the voting would be giving their assent to the treaty. Actually, as the Indians all knew, the opposite was the truth. The refusal of Indians to attend and to participate in the voting was an indication of their utter contempt for the proceedings.

That night there was much talk about what Devil's Horn had said. The next day there was more talking in the council shed. Devil's Horn talked again. The Ridges both talked. Elias Boudinot talked, and Gunter and McCoy, and there were others. Some said that what Georgia was doing to the Cherokees was not right, that it was even illegal, and that President Jackson was violating his trust, his oath of office even, by not protecting the Cherokees from Georgia. Even so, they said, they recognized the reality of their situation, and they were prepared to sign the treaty and to make the move. There were some attacks on John Ross by speakers who said that his delaying tactics were only making things worse for the Cherokees who were foolish enough to listen to him. It was a long day, full of talk—more talk.

On Thursday a white man read the proposed treaty, and it was translated into Cherokee for those who could not understand English. The translator had just begun. Nickajack heard something like, "The Cherokees are anxious to make this treaty with the United States Government because of the problems they have been having with their white neighbors and because they would like to reunite their people and secure for themselves a permanent home under their own laws and their own government." That was about as far as it had gone when Nickajack heard some crackling and smelled smoke. He looked around, then looked up. The roof of the great shed was on fire.

"Ajila!" he shouted.

"Fire!" someone else cried. There were more shouts and people ran out from under the shed.

Some men got long poles and went back underneath and poked up at the roof, knocking sections of it down, stamping on the flames when they landed on the ground. A man shinnied up one of the tall, thick corner posts, and he heaved himself up so he could look the roof over. He called back down and said that the fire was out.

Soon the people were gathered up again underneath what was left of the roof to hear the rest of the treaty translated into Cherokee. It was a long treaty, and much of it was unclear to Nickajack. There were a few ideas or phrases, however, which stuck in his mind. He remembered hearing that five million dollars was to be paid to the Cherokees for all of their lands and possessions east of the Mississippi River. He remembered hearing again that the United States Government was going to assume that any Cherokee who failed to show up at this meeting was agreeing with the proposed treaty. He heard a description of the western lands which were to be the new Cherokee Nation, but he did not understand the description.

He heard the translator say that there was a United States Army post in these new Cherokee lands called Fort Gibson, and that the United States would keep that fort, but if the United States ever abandoned the fort, then it would belong to the Cherokees. Nickajack thought that he understood the translator to say that some of those lands the

United States was giving to the Cherokees were occupied by another tribe of Indians—the Osage—and that the United States Government in this treaty promised to get those Osages out of there. Nickajack remembered hearing stories that had come back from the Cherokees who had already moved west about fighting wars with those Osages.

The treaty said that the new Cherokee Nation out in the west would never be included in the limits of any state or territory. There was a promise of perpetual peace and friendship between the citizens of the United States and the Cherokee people. There was a promise on the part of the United States to protect the Cherokee Nation from both domestic strife and foreign enemies.

The United States promised to move the Cherokees to their new homes at its own expense and to provide them with a living for one year after their arrival there. Steamboats and wagons were promised for the move. Two years time from the signing and ratification of the treaty was given to the Cherokees to complete their move. There was much more in the treaty, but Nickajack could not understand it all.

The long treaty had been read through twice, and everyone was tired. Nothing more was done that day, except for two brief speeches. Major Ridge got up to tell everyone that it was a good treaty, and

Elias Boudinot did the same. Then the meeting broke up for the day.

On Friday, December 25, a committee of twenty was appointed to carry on final negotiations with Devil's Horn. But it was Christmas Day, so the committee promised to report to the people on its negotiations with Devil's Horn the next day. The committee adjourned to the home of Elias Boudinot. Nickajack heard the names of the committee read off: There was Major Ridge, Elias Boudinot, John Gunter, John Ridge and Andrew Ross. Nickajack turned to Coffee Soldier in surprise.

"Ross?" he said.

"Yes," said Coffee. "Andrew is the brother of Chief John Ross."

From somewhere barrels of rum were produced, and many of the people began to get drunk.

"It's to celebrate Christmas," said Coffee. "Have some."

Nickajack had been to church and listened to the preachers, but he couldn't remember if Christmas was when Jesus was born or when he died or when he rose up from the dead. He was pretty sure that it was one of those days, and he didn't know what drinking rum had to do with any of them, but he drank.

On Saturday the rum was gone, and the people who had consumed it felt bad, so no business was conducted that day, and it was just as well. The committee was not yet ready to report to the people anyway. Nickajack thought that he was dying, although Coffee Soldier assured him that he was not.

On Sunday the people were lazy and sluggish. The committee did not report that day either, but the people did not seem to care. It was Monday evening when the committee finally came out of Boudinot's house and reconvened the general council underneath the shed. They recommended the treaty to the people, and the people voted their approval. The committee was then formally authorized to sign the treaty for the entire gathering, and it was understood that the gathering represented the entire Cherokee people.

On Thursday, December 29, 1835, the committee prepared for the formal signing. They took some witnesses with them back into Boudinot's house, and Coffee Soldier and Nickajack were included among the witnesses. They crowded into the parlor of Boudinot's two-story home. A fire roared in the big fireplace. The treaty was read once more, and it was time to sign. No one moved. Nickajack looked around the room. He felt as if he had been drawn into a group of conspirators, and he thought that he read guilt on all the faces there. But his impression changed abruptly, and the solemn faces looked as if they were all gathered there for a funeral.

Suddenly John Gunter stood up and moved boldly to the table where the document was laid out.

"I'm not afraid," he said. "I'll sell the whole country."

He picked up the quill and dipped it in the inkwell. He wrote his name, and the process was begun. Andrew Ross, the Chief's brother, went next. Nickajack's heart raced. He felt like— What? He could find nothing in his experience with which to compare this feeling. He was witnessing something cataclysmic, something that could lead to the end of the world.

Another man got up to sign, and then another. Nickajack did not know all these men on the committee. But he did know Major Ridge, and he watched in awe when the old man took his turn. Although his hair was completely white, Major Ridge was still a formidable presence, massive and powerful looking with piercing dark eyes. He was dressed in the manner of a plantation owner. He signed the document, and then he stood up straight, his face gone ashen.

"I have signed my death warrant," he said.

CHAPTER 8

Sitting in the courtroom five years after the event, Nickajack shuddered. It was as real, as tangible to him as the voice of the lying witness right there in the room. Time had become compressed for Nickajack. Everything that had happened was still happening. There was no past. There was only present. And in this strange, new present, he continued to relive the old events.

On December 30, the day following the signing of the treaty, the committee had reported to the general gathering once again, and the people there had given their unanimous assent to the act. It was official, and the meeting was adjourned.

People began leaving New Echota, returning to their homes. But they had no homes. They had just sold them. They had sold not only their own homes, but everyone else's as well. They had begun returning to what had been their homes to pack up whatever belongings they had in preparation for the long move to the new country in the west.

Nickajack had sought out the highest mountain ridge nearby, and he climbed up there. He stood there, staring toward the west, and he wondered how far beyond this horizon they had to travel. What was out there in the west? He knew that there were Cherokees already living in the west, and he knew that he would be moving with other Cherokees, including his good friend Coffee. Yet somehow he felt alone. He felt like an orphan. He had never known anything but this land.

"It won't be so bad," Coffee had said. "They're going to give us wagons and steamboats to ride. And they'll pay us. Money. They'll give us food and blankets and clothing for a year after we get there. And besides all that, we won't have these Georgians to worry about anymore. And we won't have those government men coming around to ask for more treaties and more land all the time. It won't be so bad."

Nickajack wasn't convinced. He remembered the expression on the face of old Major Ridge when he had signed what he called his death warrant. He remembered the tension in the room when the very people who had urged the signing of the treaty were at last faced with actually putting their names down.

Still he said nothing to Coffee about his feelings.

He kept within himself the dark sense of foreboding which had settled in deep and to stay just as—he recalled—just as he had first stepped inside the home of Elias Boudinot on that fateful day.

He had traveled most of the way back home with Coffee Soldier, and most of the way he was silent. Coffee talked. He did not seem to notice Nickajack's silence. He simply made up for it. He talked about the meeting they had just attended and the treaty that had been signed. He talked about the Ridges and Boudinot, and it was obvious that he thought of them as great men. He talked about how he would pack and how he would move, and he talked about the adventure of making such a move with his friends. He speculated about the west and about building new homes and a new country in a wilderness occupied primarily by wild Osages.

"Coffee," said Nickajack, "what is wilderness?"

"What?" said Coffee. "Well, it's— Wilderness is land where nobody lives, where no one has touched it. It's—like a virgin."

"But you said there are Osages there," said Nickajack.

"Wilderness is land where no civilization has been," said Coffee. "The Osages are wild Indians."

"What are wild Indians?"

"Wild Indians are Indians who haven't yet learned the ways of civilization the way we have."

They walked on a few more steps in silence. Then Nickajack spoke again.

"Coffee, what are the ways of civilization?"

"Ah," said Coffee. "You know that."

Nickajack put a hand on Coffee's shoulder and stopped him. They stood still for a moment.

"No, I don't know. Tell me. What are the ways of civilization?"

"Well, going to school and to church, I guess."

"Dressing up like white men?" Nickajack said. "The way we are?"

"Well, yes."

"Owning black people?"

"That's part of it."

"Buying and selling land?"

"Yes," said Coffee. "Buying and selling. Knowing who owns things."

"And putting people out of their homes," said Nickajack. "That must be civilization, too. I guess that we are civilized. We're going to put those Osage people out of their homes."

Nickajack decided to abandon the discussion which he had begun. It was beginning to make his head hurt.

"When will we move?" he said.

"I don't know," said Coffee. "Soon, I think. John Ridge will let us know. We have two years, and I guess that the committee has to go to Washington yet. They'll let us know, but I think that we should get ready."

"Yes. We should get ready."

Toward the end of their journey, they separated, each headed for his own home. Along the way, Nickajack met a neighboring family on the road. There was a man and wife and four children. The man, whose name was *Saloli,* or Squirrel, was just a few years older than Nickajack. They had been near neighbors all their lives. *Saloli* was carrying a small bundle wrapped in an old blanket. The wife was carrying a basket filled with odds and ends, and each child carried something in both hands.

" '*Siyo,*" said Nickajack. "Where are you all going?"

"To my mother-in-law's house," said *Saloli.* "If she still has one."

The man's voice was bitter, and he did not look at Nickajack as one looks at an old friend.

"What has happened?" said Nickajack.

"Some white men came and drove us out. What you see here is all they allowed us to carry away."

"Ah," said Nickajack, "the times are bad. I wonder if my own family is still in our home."

"Of course they are," said the woman. "We came by there on our way and saw them. They are quite content."

"You were with the Treaty Party," said *Saloli*. "You're in no danger. Not from the Georgians anyway. They're your friends."

Nickajack started to protest his innocence, but *Saloli* just walked on ignoring him. Besides, Nickajack wasn't quite convinced of his innocence himself. He stood in the road and watched the family slowly disappear around the bend. Finally he resumed his own trek.

*   *   *

It was almost a year and a half before they moved. Nickajack, Coffee Soldier and both their families were ready to go soon after the meeting at New Echota, and Nickajack wondered why, when the Government had been so anxious to get them out of Georgia and the other states, they were being made to wait.

"The committee had to go to Washington and wait for the treaty to be ratified by the United States Senate," said Coffee.

"What does that mean?" said Nickajack.

"The treaty is no good until the Senate says so."

"I thought that it was good when it was signed."

"No," said Coffee.

"How long does that take?"

"I don't know," said Coffee, "but they got it done. It took maybe three months. I'm not sure."

"If it's done," said Nickajack, "then why are we still waiting?"

"I guess we're waiting for the Government to give us our money and to get the boats and wagons ready for us."

"We could have walked all the way by now."

"The time will come soon enough," said Coffee.

"I don't know about that. People are threatening to kill us because of the treaty signing."

"Ah, I know. John Ross keeps them stirred up," said Coffee. "He's blaming everything on the Treaty Party. He's wrong. It would have happened anyway, but the longer we waited, the worse the terms would have been and the worse the Georgia Guard would have gotten."

Nickajack shrugged.

"I don't know," he said.

*   *   *

They gathered up in early March of 1837 at Ross's Landing, nearly five hundred of them. They were counted and their names were listed and they were paid in cash. There were white men there selling whiskey, and many of the Indians got drunk, and some of them were broke again by the time they sobered up. General Smith was in charge, and on the third day of March, he had the people herded onto eleven flatboats with all their belongings. Major Ridge was among them, and there were rumors that his health was failing. Some said he would never survive the journey. Traveling the river on the flatboats was miserable. The boats were open, and the wind was cold, but after three more days they stopped at a place called Gunter's Landing. General Smith was no longer with them. He had put another white man in charge, and that man had caused the boats to land at an island in the middle of the river. That way the Indians couldn't get to the whiskey sellers at the Landing. There a big riverboat was waiting for them.

The next day, they were loaded onto the riverboat, and they rode it as far as it could take them. When the water was too low for the big boat, they disembarked and camped. Nickajack did not know where they were, but soon a railroad train came along on iron rails. It was the first one Nickajack had ever seen, and it both frightened and amazed him. The train pulled several flat cars, much like the flat boats they had begun the journey on, and the Indians were loaded onto the flat cars.

Travel on the train was fast, but it was also frightening, loud, uncomfortable and dirty. Nickajack was glad when the train finally stopped and they were unloaded again. They camped again near another river and waited for another steamboat.

It was the thirteenth of March when the steamboat arrived. They had been traveling for ten days.

When the steamboat arrived, it had two other boats attached to it. They were not flat like the first ones they had ridden. Nickajack heard the white men and the Cherokees who talked English call them keelboats.

They rode this boat and the attached keelboats for five days. Then again they went ashore and camped. Coffee told Nickajack that the boat was too large for the river ahead. They were waiting for a smaller boat. They were in Arkansas, he said. The journey was almost over.

It was the twenty-eighth of March when the smaller boat stopped at Fort Smith and the Cherokees got off. Altogether the trip had taken twenty-five days. The white men said that the boat was going a little farther to a place called Fort Coffee. They said that the nearest way to the place some of the people planned to settle, though, was a road from Fort Smith. Major Ridge decided to leave by land from Fort Smith, and so did Coffee Soldier and, therefore, Nickajack.

The Government was still obligated to finance the trip, and so wagons and horses and mules were provided. It wasn't long before they had crossed the line into the new Cherokee Nation. Major Ridge and most of the party kept moving, but Nickajack pulled his family off to the side of the road. Coffee did the same.

"What are you doing?" said Coffee.

"I just want to stand here for a while," said Nickajack. "This is our new country."

"Yes," said Coffee. "It is. It's good land, too. Lots of water. Lots of trees and hills. It's not so different from that we had."

"No," said Nickajack. "I guess not."

"We'd better catch up with the others," said Coffee. "We're still close to Arkansas, and they said that the road in Arkansas is infested with bandits. We don't want them to catch us with just the two of us to fight."

"Howa," said Nickajack. "Let's go."

Bandits, he thought, or wild Osage Indians. He wondered if they would have to fight for this new land. The Government said that it belonged to them, but he doubted if bandits and wild Indians cared much about what the Government said. The United States Government had promised the Cherokees peace and protection if they would move west. Nickajack wondered if the Government would be able to keep that promise. He wondered if they would even try. Then he wondered what was happening back in the old country.

He knew that John Ross had refused to recognize the Treaty of New Echota as a valid treaty. He did not recognize the gathering there at New Echota as a valid national council. They said that Ross was still maintaining his same old position. He was telling the people to hold out. He was saying that the

United States could not make them move. As a result, they said, the people back east were suffering more and more every day. Some said that Ross was just trying to hold out for more money, that he was looking for ways of lining his own pockets.

Nickajack did not want to believe that about the man who was supported by an overwhelming majority of the Cherokee people. Four or five hundred had been at New Echota to show support for the Ridges. That was four or five hundred out of perhaps eighteen thousand Cherokees. No. He did not want to believe that Chief Ross was anything but honest, and he knew that some people on the other side had also accused the Ridges of selfish motives for their actions. Nickajack wasn't sure what the truth might be. He had made the move because of his friendship for Coffee, not for any political reasons. He wondered if it might not be true that both John Ross and the Ridges were honest, and they simply saw things differently from each other.

He knew, however, the feelings of those he had joined, and he tried to avoid any political discussions. When he found himself in the middle of one, he just listened, grunted and occasionally nodded his head.

But eighteen thousand Cherokees . . . what was happening to them while he and these four hundred or so casually looked over this new country in the west? He thought of the family of his onetime friend *Saloli* turned out of their own home, wandering homeless, hoping to find someone still relatively secure who would take them in. Would they find anyone? How could anyone remain secure back there with the Georgia Guard running wild, with greedy Georgians and other whites turned loose on them and no law to protect Cherokees? How could the property or even the lives of any Cherokees back there be safe?

Nickajack felt a pang of guilt for being among the even temporarily secure, but as with other feelings, he kept this one to himself.

CHAPTER 9

Nickajack and Coffee Soldier each received a canvas tent from the Indian agent at Fort Gibson. They pitched their tents outside the fort near the river. With their families thus minimally established, they went back to the fort to see what they could discover about the new country. There was a great deal of activity inside the fort. Newly arrived immigrants were lined up to see the Indian agent for rations. Others, like Nickajack and Coffee Soldier, wandered aimlessly, looking at whatever was there to be seen. Some few gave strong indications that they had discovered the secret lurking places of the whiskey peddlers. The whole place seemed to Nickajack and Coffee to be too busy. They were about to give up and leave when Coffee noticed two men off by themselves leaning against the stockade fence. One was a soldier in uniform. The other, smoking a pipe, was dressed in frontiersman's buckskins with the colorful Cherokee additions of a woven sash around the waist and a turban wrapped around his head.

"Let's go over there," said Coffee. They walked toward the two men, and as they drew closer, Coffee said, "He looks like a half-breed." The "half-breed" saw them coming.

" *'Siyo,* " he said, but then he switched to English. "Are you new arrivals?"

"Yes," said Coffee. "My name is Coffee Soldier. This is my friend Nickajack."

"I'm Jack Spaniard, but most folks call me Spanish Jack," said the smoker. "This here is a friend of mine, Lieutenant John Woods from Vermont. Have you just arrived?"

"We came to Fort Smith on a boat," said Coffee. "Then we got horses and wagons and came here. Our families are out there in tents right now. We need to decide where to build our houses."

"Just pick out a spot you like," said Spanish Jack, "as long as no one else is there."

"There's lots of room," said Woods.

"You mean we could just build houses—right where we have those tents?" said Coffee.

"I suppose you could," said Woods, giving Spanish Jack an inquiring look and waiting for his nod of agreement, "but I wouldn't recommend it."

"I wouldn't either," said Spanish Jack. "No offense to my friend here, but who wants to live by an army post?"

"He's right," said Woods. "Do you have children?"

"We both have," said Coffee.

"It can get rough around here," said the lieutenant. "The army gets all kinds of men, including some of the worst kind. Then an army post always seems to attract the whiskey sellers. We try to control it, but we can't seem to catch them all."

"Some Indians get it too," said Spanish Jack. "And it will only get worse. When the rest of the people come out from the east, they'll all be coming through here. I'd ride north a couple of days if I was you."

Coffee Soldier ran his hands through his hair. He turned and looked off toward the north, even though his view was blocked by buildings and by the stockade fence.

"North, huh?" he said.

"It's just a suggestion," said Spanish Jack.

"Well," said Coffee, "it's the only suggestion we got."

Spanish Jack looked at Nickajack, who had not spoken a word. Nickajack smiled.

"Yonegas hiwonisgi?" said Spanish Jack, asking if Nickajack could speak English.

Nickajack shook his head. "A little," he said. "I understand."

"Good," said Spanish Jack. "I was afraid we were leaving you out."

"I understand," repeated Nickajack. "Okay." But then he spoke to Spanish Jack in Cherokee. "Are you one of the Early Settlers?"

"Yes," said Jack. "I've lived out here most of my life. We have our own government. We call it the Cherokee Nation West. Our chief is John Brown, *Uwodige.*"

"Then I guess *Uwodige* is our chief now, too," said Coffee.

"You know," said Spanish Jack, "I'm going north in the morning on business. If you like, ride along with me."

"Just hope he doesn't run across any Osages along the way if you do," said Woods.

"Is the war with the Osages still going on?" asked Coffee.

"No," said Woods. "It's over. But the war between the Osages and Spanish Jack here is a different matter."

"Ah, Lieutenant," protested Spanish Jack, "you don't trust me. I told you that I'd quit killing those Osages, didn't I?"

"I know you too well, Spaniard," said Woods. "Too, too well."

*   *   *

They left at daybreak, Jack Spaniard and Coffee Soldier riding horses, Nickajack riding the white mule he had acquired at Fort Smith. Coffee and Nickajack had decided to leave their families at Fort Gibson until they had located suitable homesites. Spanish Jack said that the two men should be back to their families in five days, six at the most. They rode north out of Fort Gibson, heading farther into the new Cherokee Nation. Spanish Jack carried a long rifle, a brace of pistols, a large hunting knife and a belt ax. Coffee Soldier carried his rifle. Nickajack's old pistol was tucked into the waistband of his trousers.

The countryside was alive with new green growth. Nickajack looked around as they rode, trying to take it all in, trying to memorize, not just the route for their return trip, but everything he could about his new homeland. He recognized oak, elm, black gum, walnut, hickory, locust, dogwood, sassafras and birch trees. He knew the berry bushes that he saw along the way: huckleberry, dewberry, blackberry. And the birds he saw he recognized and knew by name. They were the same birds he had known before. Perhaps, after all, he thought, it would not be so different, not be so bad.

*   *   *

It was midmorning of their second day of riding when they met the Osages, five of them riding big strong horses. They rode abreast, effectively blocking the road for northbound traffic. As they drew closer together, Nickajack felt his heartbeat increase. So, he thought, these are wild Indians. This is what they look like. All five Osages had shaven heads with scalplocks growing from the center of the top of the head and flowing down their backs. One, apparently their leader, rode in the center and slightly ahead of the others. He was almost naked. He wore skin moccasins and a breechcloth. An eagle feather was tied in his scalplock behind his head. His ears were slit and tied with colorful bits of yarn. Around his neck was a necklace of bear claws and a United States Government peace medal hanging from red and yellow ribbons. His upper arms were braceleted in broad straps of bronze. Narrower bracelets hung loose around his wrists. Thin stripes of vermilion paint decorated his face and body seemingly at random, giving him the appearance at a glance of having suffered recent slashing from a knife. A broad, flat war club with an embedded steel blade dangled from a thin belt around his waist, and he carried at the ready a long rifle, similar to that of Spanish Jack.

The other four were similarly attired and decorated except that each of them wore buckskin leggings, and the paint and jewelry was unique to each. One had a pistol in his belt. One other held a short-barreled flintlock rifle. The three without guns had bows and wore quivers of arrows slung on their backs. All had war clubs and knives. They sat upon their horses, haughty and arrogant, and they halted at the last moment. Spanish Jack, Coffee Soldier and Nickajack stopped too, facing the Osages.

"*Bonjour, Jacques,*" said the naked Osage. "*Comment allez-vous? Eh?*"

"*Çà va,*" said Spanish Jack. "*Et vous, Le Soldat du Chêne?*"

"*Très bien, Espagnol,*" said the Osage. "*Où vous allez?*"

"*Du nord. Nord-est. C'est à savoir,*" said Spaniard. Then he spoke in Cherokee to Nickajack and Coffee. "They're Osage," he said. "The one who's talking French to me is called *Le Soldat du Chêne,* the Soldier of the Oaks."

"You know each other?" asked Coffee.

"Oh, yes," said Spanish Jack. "We're old—acquaintances."

"Will you fight?" said Nickajack.

Spanish Jack shrugged, but even while he spoke to his companions, he kept his eyes on the Soldier of the Oaks, his thumb on the hammer of his flintlock.

"*Eh, Jacques,*" said the big Osage, "*qui sont ces deux avec vous, uh?*"

"*Mes amis,*" said Spanish Jack. "*Cherokees. Bien, nous allons nos chemin. Adieu, Le Soldat du Chêne.*"

Spanish Jack urged his mount forward, and Nick-

ajack thought for a moment that he would collide
with the big Osage, but just in time to allow him to
pass, *Le Soldat du Chêne* moved aside. The Osages
left room for the Cherokees to ride on through, but
in single file. Nickajack was the last one through,
and he and Coffee Soldier hurried up to ride beside
Spanish Jack.

"Get on ahead of me," said Spaniard.

They did, and Spanish Jack looked back over his
shoulder just as *Le Soldat du Chêne* shouted something in his language. As he shouted, he whirled and
raised his rifle, but Spanish Jack's reaction was fast
and his shot was true. *Le Soldat du Chêne* cried out
as the lead ball smashed his sternum. His rifle fell
from his hands unfired, and he toppled backwards
off his horse. Spanish Jack tossed his rifle aside and
pulled out his pistols, one in each hand. Not waiting
to give the four remaining confused and indecisive
Osages time to think, he charged. His first pistol
shot smashed the right shoulder of the one with the
short rifle. The one with the pistol had pulled out
his weapon and was thumbing back the hammer
when Spanish Jack fired his second pistol. The ball
tore into the Osage's side causing his shot to go
wild. The two remaining Osages turned their
mounts and fled.

Nickajack watched the whole scene with fascinated horror, and the horror grew as Spanish Jack
dismounted and finished off the two wounded men

with his knife, then moved from one body to another to secure the scalps. The triumphant Cherokee warrior then gathered up the fallen Osages' weapons, and with those and his bloody trophies, climbed back on his horse.

"*Inena,*" he said. "Let's go."

*   *   *

Spanish Jack led them across a river which he identified as the Illinois. The water was low where they crossed, and he told them that it was usually like that. There would be a few times in a year, following heavy rains, when one would not be able to cross. He told them how to reach the nearby settlement of Park Hill, although he added that he could not think why anyone would want to go there. It was inhabited by missionaries. He led them a few more miles north and showed them the sites he had in mind. Another road, not much more than a lane, wound off toward the east. A few miles down that road, said Spanish Jack, toward Arkansas, a mixed-blood Cherokee Old Settler named Eli Johnson had a trading post. He would buy furs, surplus crops and sometimes even farm animals. And any staples one might need could be purchased from Johnson.

"If I was looking for a new place to build," he said, "this is where I'd come."

He said good-by and left them there. Nickajack

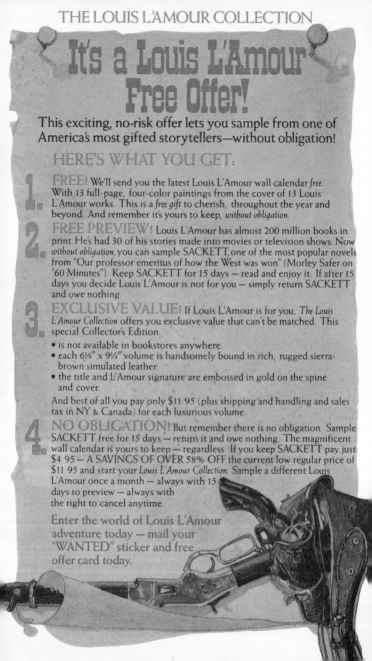

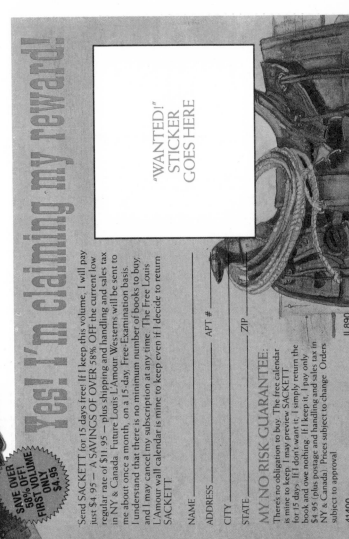

Track down and capture exciting western adventure from one of America's foremost novelists!

• It's free! • No obligation! • Exclusive value!

and Coffee Soldier stood and watched him ride away, still going north. Nickajack wondered what business it was that was taking Spanish Jack north. He had never said. How far north, he wondered, was the man going? Was he on an Osage killing trip? Nickajack wondered if the Cherokees' war with the Osages was really over. He had almost begun to feel good about the move to the west, but suddenly he was not so sure. They had left their old homes, their ancestral homes, the only homes they had ever known, to escape the growing violence from the Georgians. Had they done so, he asked himself, only to exchange that violence for this Osage war?

"Spanish Jack was right," said Coffee Soldier, interrupting Nickajack's thoughts. "This is a good place."

*   *   *

They located their homesites within easy walking distance of each other, yet the two spots were separated by thick woods, so that from either place it would seem as if there were no close neighbors. Each site was selected to provide a good spot for a house and land relatively easy to clear for planting. It would not be really easy, they knew, for the soil was rocky, and rocks were scattered across the top of the land in profusion. They used the loose rocks to stack and mark off the places where they would build and the places they would clear. Together they planned the two homes. They would work together, at least until both houses were complete, both fields cleared and plowed and fences built at both homesites. In the excitement of the planning, the Osages were almost forgotten.

*   *   *

Back at Fort Gibson at their temporary tent homes, the two families had a lively reunion.

"We're going to build a new house?" said one of the children.

"Two new houses," said Nickajack. "One for each family."

The wives and children were anxious to get started so they could see their new homesites.

"When will we go?" asked Coffee's wife.

"In the morning we'll go to the agent," said Coffee. "We'll see if we can get tools and supplies. After that we'll leave this place and go to our new homes."

The women prepared a meal over open fires built out in front of the tents, and they were just about ready to sit down and eat when Lieutenant John Woods came walking up.

"Good evening," he said. "I see you made it back all right."

"Yes," said Coffee.

"Did you find a suitable place?"

"Yes, we did. Eat with us, and then we'll tell you all about it."

Woods glanced back toward the fort and considered for a moment before he answered.

"Yes, thank you," he said. "I will."

He sat down and ate with them, and when they were finished, the three men sat and had more coffee.

"Spanish Jack showed us a good place," said Coffee. "Two good places close together. He said if he was looking for a place, that would be his choice. We marked it with stones, and now we're going back with our families to build and to settle. It's across a river from here, two days' ride, near a place called Park Hill."

"The Illinois River?" said Woods.

"Yes. Spanish Jack called it the Illinois."

"I'm glad for you," said Woods. "I know this hasn't been an easy thing for you to do, to leave your homes and move out here to a new country. I hope all goes well for all of you from here on."

"Thank you," said Coffee.

Nickajack was not taking part in the conversation, but he understood most of what was being said. He was puzzled by the attitude and behavior of this white man. He seemed to be a good man. And it had also seemed apparent when they had met him that he and Spanish Jack were friends. All of Nickajack's previous experience with white men had been bad. And this one even wore the hated uniform of the United States Army. Perhaps the white men, like the Cherokees, did not all agree with each other. It was difficult to believe that this was the same sort of man as those members of the Georgia Guard who had ransacked Cherokee homes and brutalized Cherokee people.

He noticed that the lieutenant's cup was empty, and he got up to refill it. He wasn't confident enough about his English to converse, but he could show the man that he was not being intentionally unfriendly.

"Thank you," said Woods, accepting the refill. "So when did you last see my old friend Spaniard?"

"He rode on north after he showed us our home-sites," said Coffee.

Nickajack thought about the encounter with the Osages, but he said nothing. He noticed that a worried look came over the young lieutenant's face, and he thought that this man really cared for Spanish Jack. The sun was low in the western sky, and Lieutenant Woods got up to leave. He thanked them for their hospitality and wished them well again. Then he started walking toward the fort.

"I think that man has been watching us," said Nickajack's wife.

"Watching us?" said Nickajack.

"I mean while you were gone."

Nickajack and Coffee looked at one another.

"He said that it was rough around here," said Coffee. "He said that it was not a good place for children. He was looking out for our families while we were away."

*   *   *

In the morning they went to the agent's office in the fort. In the five days they had been away, the rush had subsided, and they were able to get in to see the agent after just a short wait. They told him they had located their homesites, and he issued them supplies and farm tools. They even got some cows and pigs.

"This will be a good start," said Coffee.

"Yes," said Nickajack. "It will be."

CHAPTER 10

They moved their families to the homesites they had selected, and there they set up the tents for temporary shelter. They let the cows run loose in the fields and the pigs in the woods, and then they started work by locating and felling suitable trees for the log homes they had planned. They cut the logs for cabins that would be thirty feet long and twenty feet deep, and they built the first one at Coffee Soldier's place. Both families lived together in the one cabin, still making use of the two tents, while construction continued. They built the second cabin at Nickajack's place, and the families separated. They were not far apart, of course, and the two men continued to work together. They cleared their fields next and prepared for planting, and they built fences. Then they built two more cabins, one beside each of the others. Each home was finished so that there were two cabins side by side connected by a common roof. In one cabin were a kitchen and a family room. The other was the bedroom. The space between the cabins, called a dog run, served as a cool, shaded place to sit on summer days.

There was always more work to be done, but when both two-cabin houses were built, they felt like their new homes were finished. At last they felt like they once more had a place where they belonged. They had laid in their first crop, when Nickajack and Coffee decided to pay a visit to Eli Johnson.

*   *   *

"How's the work progressing?" asked Johnson.

"The houses and the fences are done," said Coffee. "The fields are cleared and crops are planted. We're not settlers anymore. We're just working farmers."

"That's good," said Johnson. "Are you going to the big council?"

Nickajack and Coffee looked at one another.

"I don't know," said Coffee. "We haven't heard about it."

"Oh," said Johnson, "it's going to be a big council of all the Indian tribes in this country: Cherokee, Creek, Seminole, Seneca, Delaware, Shawnee, Quapaw, Sac, maybe more. Hosted by the Cherokees down at Double Springs."

"No Osages?" said Nickajack.

"I don't think so," said Johnson. "I don't know if they were invited, and even if they were, I don't think they'd come. Besides, they've moved north of here now."

"Where is Double Springs?" asked Coffee.

"South of Fort Gibson."

"That's a long ways to go, and we have work to do," said Nickajack.

"Are you going?" asked Coffee.

"I'm not sure," said Johnson. "I'm thinking about it. I've never seen that many different kinds of Indians in one place. I'd like to go, but I have to keep my store open. If I can talk my wife into keeping the store while I'm gone, I might go. The trouble is, if I go, she'll want to go."

"What's the purpose of this meeting?" said Nickajack.

"I don't know," said Johnson. "I think it's just to declare peace and friendship. It's just that kind of meeting, I think. You know, new neighbors getting acquainted. No special other reason. The funny thing is that the soldiers at Fort Gibson and the white people over in Arkansas think that it's going to be a big war council. They're all afraid that we're going to have a big uprising and wipe them out."

"What makes them think that?" said Coffee.

"I don't know. They just think that's the only reason Indians ever meet, I guess."

"I've been to lots of meetings," said Nickajack. "Mostly they do nothing. I've never been to war."

Coffee Soldier rubbed a hand over his chin and looked thoughtful. He was studying a new saddle which was displayed there on a sawhorse. He put a hand on the horn and with the other hand lovingly patted the leather on the seat.

"When is this meeting?" he said.

"In about two weeks, I think," said Johnson.

"Maybe we could get ready," said Coffee, looking at Nickajack. "Maybe we should go to this meeting."

"I don't know," said Nickajack.

"Sure," said Coffee. "We could take our families. I'd like to see all those Indians, too."

"I'll talk to my wife," said Johnson. "Maybe we can just close the store for a few days. We could all go. She might go for that. I went to the last council without her."

"When was that?" asked Coffee.

"Not long ago," said Johnson. "It wasn't a big one. It was just Cherokees. Right after you came. You were probably busy building your houses. It was our Chief and Council and your leaders: Major Ridge, John Ridge and Elias Boudinot. Some others."

Johnson went on to tell them about the previous

meeting. Chief John Brown was there with his Assistant Chief John Looney and the tribal council of the Cherokee Nation West. Representing the recent immigrants were the two Ridges, Elias Boudinot, John Bell and other treaty signers. There were large numbers of observers as well from both groups, according to Johnson. Chief Brown had started the meeting out with a welcome. The Cherokee Nation West, he said, was pleased to receive the recent immigrants. He was happy to report that the much discussed troubles with the Osages were for all practical purposes at an end. The United States had negotiated a treaty with the Osages whereby that tribe had agreed to remove north. When Nickajack heard this, he thought of the five Osages he and Coffee had encountered with Spanish Jack. He gave Coffee a glance, but said nothing. Johnson went on with his story of the council. Chief Brown had expressed his sorrow at what was happening back east in the old Cherokee country, but he said that was the reason that he and his people had moved west in the first place.

"With the new territory mapped out for us by the United States," he had said, "there will be plenty of room for all Cherokees. We have learned to love this country, and I think that you will too."

Then he explained their form of government, which, he said, was like the old government in the east before the development of the written constitution. Then he had stepped down, and Major Ridge had been invited to speak, but the old man had deferred to his son. John Ridge told the assembly that the new immigrants appreciated the warm welcome afforded them by the Early Settlers and assured Chief Brown and all others gathered there that no one in his family had any further political ambitions. The new immigrants would be content, he said, more than content, to live under the government established by the Early Settlers. He too expressed sorrow at the events in the old Cherokee Nation. It was sad, he said, that John Ross had deluded the mass of the people into thinking that they would be able to stay in their homes. It was Ross, Ridge said, who was to blame for all the suffering of the majority of the poor and ignorant Cherokees. And, he said, while he and the other immigrants were perfectly willing to live under the government of the Cherokee Nation West, he could not say what would happen when John Ross and the majority of the Cherokee people finally would arrive.

Others had spoken, Johnson said, but the speeches of Chief Brown and John Ridge had set the tone of the meeting, and after those two had spoken, nothing new had been said. Nickajack and Coffee took that as official confirmation that their government was now the government of the Early

Settlers, the Cherokee Nation West. They were satisfied, and Johnson had finished his tale.

"How much do you want for this saddle?" said Coffee.

*   *   *

A week and a day passed, and the three families packed for their trip south. Nickajack and Coffee each brought their canvas tents. They took dried meat and cornmeal, and they packed what few extra clothes they had. Nickajack was surprised to discover that he enjoyed the trip. It was a leisurely trip with a known destination and purpose, and it was good to get better acquainted with the Johnsons. Nickajack remembered the trail all the way down to Fort Gibson, and by the time they got there, they had traveled two days and camped one night. It was late in the afternoon when they arrived at the fort, so they decided to camp there for the night and go on down to Double Springs in the morning. They had set up their tents and built small cooking fires, when they saw a rider coming toward them.

"Look," said Nickajack. "Look who's coming."

"Spanish Jack," said Coffee.

Spaniard rode up closer to the tents before he called out.

" 'Siyo, my friends," he said. "Are you on the way to Double Springs?"

"Yes," said Johnson. "Get down off your horse and eat with us."

*   *   *

After they had eaten, the men settled back to smoke and talk.

"Did you get your homes built?" asked Spanish Jack.

"Yes," said Nickajack. "Right where you showed us. Stop to see us sometime when you're traveling by."

"Are you going to the meeting?" asked Johnson.

"I'll go down there to see who shows up," said Spanish Jack.

"The Osages aren't invited, I think," said Johnson. Nickajack and Coffee gave each other a quick glance.

"I'll just look in," said Spanish Jack. "Have you heard the news from the east?"

"What news?" said Coffee.

"Soldiers are rounding up Cherokees like cattle and putting them in pens. When they get them all gathered up, they're going to march them all out here with us. They said that people look back over their shoulders as the soldiers are marching them away, and they see their houses in flames. There was a deaf Cherokee man who turned the wrong way, and the soldiers shot him to death. The Georgians are drawing lots to see which piece of Cherokee land they own."

*   *   *

The next morning, Spanish Jack rode with them on down to Double Springs. The crowds were already gathering. Many of the Cherokee men there wore colorful turbans, hunting jackets and woven sashes. The women wore their tear dresses, so called because the cloth was torn, not cut with scissors, in the making. Some, though, were dressed in the fashion of the typical white frontiersmen and women, and fewer still were well-dressed in the manner of successful businessmen or plantation owners.

The hunting jackets of the Creek men were similar to those of the Cherokees, except that some of them were longer, and the Creeks seemed to display more silver ornamentation. In place of turbans, some of them wore cloth caps with silver bands. The Seminoles were the most strikingly unique, their men in their knee length shirts, their turbans decorated with the long feathers of exotic swamp birds. Some of the Seminole women wore bright dresses of multicolored patchwork cloth.

The Sacs wore small fur caps with single eagle feathers sticking straight up behind. They wore buckskin leggings and shirts bought or bartered from white men. Many of them were wrapped in blankets, usually bright red. They wore bear claw necklaces and brass or silver armbands. Some of the men had shaved heads topped off with red roaches. Their women wore either buckskin dresses or cloth dresses acquired from white traders. The Delawares, Quapaws, and Shawnees seemed to Nickajack to be attired in various combinations of the same items worn by the others. It was a lively and colorful gathering. Nickajack was as fascinated by the babble of languages as he was by the visual variety.

Speeches were made by representatives of each tribe, and the translations seemed endless, but all of it boiled down to repeated pledges of peace and friendship. That was what Eli Johnson had told them to expect. It was good to know that they would be at peace with their neighboring tribes, but Nickajack kept thinking about what Spanish Jack had told them of the events in the east, and he wondered what would happen when John Ross and all the other Cherokees arrived in the Cherokee Nation West. Would the talk still be of friendship and peace? He wondered, but he kept his doubts to himself.

With the day drawing to a close, the official activities came to an end. Then there was much visiting and much feasting, and a little later, Nickajack could hear the sounds of a drum. Then came a high-pitched singing of a style he had not heard before. There was a crowd gathered around a fire off at some distance, and it seemed that the strange music was coming from there.

"That's where those Sacs are camped," said Coffee. "Let's go see."

"Can we go too?" said one of the children.

"Let's all go," said Nickajack.

They walked over to the crowd, toward the sounds, and Nickajack could feel the drumbeat in his own breast. They moved closer still, and the drums and the voices grew louder. As they made their way through the crowd, they could see the Sac men around the drum. Others were dancing, men and women both, even small children. The dancing, like the singing, was strange to Nickajack. The men, bedecked with feathers, seemed to move like birds. Some others, not Sac, joined in and did their best to imitate the movements of the Sacs. At last the children of Nickajack followed by those of Coffee Soldier ran to join the circle.

It was like that for four days and four nights, the speeches in the daytime, the dancing and singing late into the night. Then the meeting broke up, and everyone headed for home.

"Coffee," said Nickajack as they were moving north again, "those singers and dancers, were those wild Indians?"

CHAPTER 11

The first ones arrived in the summer of 1838. The United States Army had begun its forced removal with about five thousand Cherokees. Those who survived the trip were a pitiful lot. They had been taken from stockades in which some of them had been held for two or three months. Many were sick before they even began the trip. They had been taken from the stockades to a place on the Hiwassee River in Tennessee and from there to Ross's Landing and then to Gunter's Landing in Alabama on the Tennessee River. There they had been loaded onto steamboats and taken to the Ohio River and to the Mississippi. From there they walked. The summer had been hot and sultry, and many of the sick had died. More had become ill along the way. The very old and the very young had suffered the most, and the death toll had been great.

Nickajack had not been at Fort Gibson to witness the arrival of this wretched mob, but one who had seen them traveled north and told the tale to Eli Johnson at his store. Johnson retold it to Nickajack one day.

"This is what the man told me," he said.

I've seen sorry looking people in my life, one or two at a time, but I tell you, I never seen a whole bunch like that at once before. I don't know how many of them was there, but they told me it was a heap less than when they started.

I talked to one man told me he'd been home a-plowing in his field. The soldiers came. They caught him up and held him, and some went on to his house. His wife was in there with their four children, and the soldiers got her and two of the young'uns, but the other two run screaming into the woods. That was at least three months ago, he said, and he ain't seen hide nor hair of them since.

He told me they was penned up like a bunch of cows for two months at least. He'd lost track of time. Some of the women, he said, went out with soldiers for a drink of whiskey. He seen some get sick and die right there. Then when they brought them on out here, he said, they buried someone pert near every day along the way. Sometimes four or five a day.

He said he'd cried so much, he thought that he could never cry no more.

But no more came. And there were fifteen thousand more, at least, back east. Nickajack went on about his work, but he almost constantly thought about John Ross and the rest of the Cherokees. He wondered what was happening back there. Maybe John Ross had been right, and they would never come. Maybe they would, after all, be able to stay in their old homes. If not, he wondered, when would they arrive, and if they came, he wondered, what would happen next?

Then Spanish Jack had stopped by for a visit. Nickajack thought that he saw fresh scalps hanging from Spaniard's saddle, but he didn't say anything about them. He invited Spaniard in to eat, and after the meal, they talked. For a while they made small talk. Nickajack carefully avoided any questions about the nature of Spaniard's business to the north.

"Have you been to Fort Gibson lately?" he finally asked.

"I was there just before I went north," said Spaniard.

"Have any more Cherokees come west?"

"Not the last I knew," said Spaniard. "From what I heard, John Ross has taken a new approach with the United States. I guess he knows his cause is hopeless now, and the move was so bad for the ones the soldiers brought out here, that Ross has told the Government that the Cherokees can move themselves and do a better job of it. I guess they think he's right. The latest news I heard, he's haggling with them about the cost."

"About the cost?" said Nickajack.

"The United States is supposed to pay for the move," said Spaniard, "so if the Cherokees manage it for themselves, the United States Government will pay them to do it."

"Oh," said Nickajack, "I see. So when will they come?"

"Who knows? When John Ross gets his price, I guess."

* * *

The first seven hundred or so arrived in January of 1839 after one hundred and twenty-six days of travel. Their Cherokee conductor was Elijah Hicks. There had been thirty-four deaths along the way. Seven days later the next group arrived. Under the leadership of John Benge, they had been one hundred and six days making the trip, with thirty-three deaths out of over a thousand immigrants. Hair Conrad's contingent of about seven hundred was next in about six more days. Along the way they had lost fifty-four to death, twenty-four by desertion, in one hundred and forty-six days of travel. And the month of January closed with nearly three thousand immigrants having arrived in the Cherokee Nation West.

February brought three more waves. The first, led by *Situwake,* arrived on the second day of the month after having traveled one hundred and forty-nine days. Numbering over twelve hundred, they suffered seventy-one deaths on the trail. Captain Old Field brought his eight or nine hundred in on the twenty-third. In one hundred and fifty-three days, they had lost fifty-seven by death, ten by desertion. And on the twenty-seventh, Reverend Jesse Bushyhead arrived with nearly nine hundred more. They had been traveling one hundred and seventy-eight days. Thirty-eight had died along the way. One hundred and forty-eight deserted.

The rest arrived in March in seven different groups. On the first, *Chuwaluka* brought his in, around a thousand. On the second Moses Daniel brought another thousand. On the fifth James Brown came in with seven hundred. On the fourteenth another thousand came led by George Hicks. On the eighteenth John Drew brought in two hundred, Richard Taylor nine hundred on the twenty-fourth, and the last fourteen hundred or so came with Peter Hildebrand on the twenty-fifth.

There were thirteen waves in all. In a three-month period, well over ten thousand new residents had poured into the new Cherokee Nation. At least sixteen hundred had died along the way. One of the many casualties had been *Quatie* Ross, the wife of the Principal Chief. They began calling it the Trail Where They Cried.

*   *   *

Sitting beside Colonel Walker in the courtroom while his fate was being decided by strangers, Nickajack was probably the least interested party present. He heard less than half of what was being said, and of what he did hear, he understood little, for he was not paying attention. His mind was on the past, recalling all it could of events which had led him to this place. The current debate seemed to him to be of no significance. The outcome was predetermined, and his life had already ended. To Nickajack there was no longer past or future. All time was with him in the present, and all that was left for him to do was reflect and search for answers to the puzzle that his life had become.

He had not witnessed the arrival of the waves of immigrants in 1839. He had heard about it all at various times from different people, in bits and pieces, out of order, but at last the pieces had come together in proper order in his mind.

*   *   *

So the Trail of Tears had ended, and Chief John Ross and Elias Boudinot and others had settled at Park Hill. Then Nickajack began hearing other things, things that gave him a sense of impending disaster, the kinds of things that had been nagging at a far corner of his mind for some time. John Ross and his followers insisted that the Cherokee Nation had been moved whole and complete. The Cherokee Nation as it had existed in the east had simply been transported to a new location. Nothing had changed except the location. The government was the same. John Ross was still the chief, and the old council from the east was still the council. The western lands which the United States Government had designated for the Cherokees would be governed by Principal Chief John Ross and his council.

But the Old Settlers had their own government, and they had been in the west for several generations. They had no intention of disbanding their government, and the Ridges and their followers had allied themselves with the Old Settlers when they had arrived. So now there were two Cherokee governments in the same country, and the feelings between them were bad.

"There's going to be trouble," Nickajack said one day to Coffee Soldier.

"John Ross has brought the trouble," said Coffee. "He wants to take over the government."

"I don't know," said Nickajack. "He has a different government. His is the government we have always had. We had it before all the trouble. Now it's out here in the west."

"We have two governments, but we have only one country," said Coffee. "John Ross and his people are in the Cherokee Nation West now, and they should live under the government of the Cherokee Nation West."

Nickajack thought that the treaty was supposed to reunite the Cherokee people. There should be no east and west. There should only be the Cherokee Nation. But he didn't say that. He didn't want to argue politics with his old friend.

"If we don't get some rain soon," he said, "the crops will be poor this year."

*   *   *

Another meeting was called at Double Springs in June of 1839, and Nickajack allowed Coffee to talk him into going. Six thousand Cherokees were there. They camped and visited. New immigrants mixed with Old Settlers. Some found relatives they had not seen in years. For several days it was nothing more than an informal gathering. Then the Ridges came, old Major Ridge and his son John, Elias Boudinot and his brother Stand Watie. Nickajack heard someone say, "The Ridges are here," and another answered, "They came to sell our country." He noticed that the Ridges stood apart. No one seemed to want to associate with them. At last Coffee walked over to greet them, and Nickajack followed. They shook hands all around.

"We don't seem to be welcome here," said Major Ridge.

"This is a meeting for all Cherokees," said Coffee. "Both governments are here. We're going to join together. That's the reason for this meeting."

"Yes," said John Ridge, "but you can see the way they look at us."

"They think you've come to sell this land," said Nickajack. "I heard them say so."

"We're only here to observe," said Boudinot. "We have no official business here."

Nickajack nodded toward the crowd.

"They won't believe that, I think," he said.

"He's right," said Major Ridge. "Our presence here can only lead to trouble. Come on. Let's go."

When the Ridges were gone, Nickajack stood silent for a moment. Then he spoke to Coffee.

"Maybe we should go, too," he said.

"No," said Coffee. "It's all right. We don't have to go."

So Nickajack stayed, against his better judgment. At last the meeting started, and Chief John Brown got up to speak. He welcomed the recent immigrants to the Cherokee Nation West. He welcomed them as brothers. They had been separated too long, he said, but now at last they were reunited as one nation. Other similar speeches were made from both sides, and Nickajack thought that maybe everything would be all right after all. He and Coffee had managed to work their way to the front of the crowd, where they stood very near the speakers. Then John Brown spoke to John Ross, and though he spoke privately, Nickajack overheard.

"I think our purpose here has been accomplished," said Brown. "We can adjourn."

"I don't believe my people are yet satisfied," said Ross. "They need more assurances from you. Just what is their status here?"

"I thought that I had made that clear," said Brown, "and judging from their reactions, I thought that they were satisfied."

"I think you need to be more specific," said Ross. "These people have suffered a great deal. They need to hear specific assurances from you."

"All right," said Brown. He moved back to the speaker's stand to address the crowd again. He welcomed the recent immigrants again, and he assured them that they could go anywhere in the new country they wanted to go so long as they respected the rights of others and obeyed the laws. He told them that they were full citizens with voting rights and the right to run for any public office. There would be an election in October, he said, and he expected the new immigrants to be full participants in that process.

"There are too many of them," Coffee whispered to Nickajack. "They'll take over the government."

When John Brown finished his speech, he received a hearty round of applause and cheers. The crowd of mostly new immigrants seemed well pleased. But then John Ross moved back behind the speaker's stand.

"My friends," he said, "we are pleased to be so warmly received here, and what we have just heard sounds good. But I feel compelled to point out to you, that if we should disband our formal governmental structure, the United States Government, which is obligated to us for all that we have lost, may never meet those obligations."

"I understand your point," said Brown. "Then keep your government together for purposes of dealing with the United States regarding your claims."

"That's not enough," said Ross. "We are used to living under a more sophisticated form of government than that which you have here."

"Our government is modeled after yours," said Brown. "The laws are the same. Keep your government the way it is to deal with the United States. Then in October you can run for every office that we have. You outnumber us by two to one at least. If all your people vote, you'll win the seats."

"We can't afford to take the chance," said Ross.

"The United States might consider that our government has been dissolved unless we continue it without a break."

*   *   *

The meeting lasted for ten days, and nothing was resolved. Nickajack went home determined to attend no more of them. He would stay at home with his family and attend to his business. Let government do the work of government. He need not be involved. It was not long after that, still in the month of June, when Nickajack, at home, heard the pounding of horse's hooves outside his house. He hurried to the door and opened it, and there was Coffee Soldier riding up fast. Coffee reined in his mount just in front of the door.

"Have you heard the news?" he shouted.

"No," said Nickajack. "I haven't heard anything."

Coffee dismounted and dropped the reins.

"They've killed them," he said. "Major Ridge, John Ridge and Boudinot are dead."

"Who killed them?" said Nickajack.

"There was a secret meeting," said Coffee, "after the big meeting broke up. Some of Ross's people. They decided that those men must die for selling the country back east. They also said those men had caused the meeting to go bad. They went to John

Ridge's house, maybe twenty-five of them, and they dragged him from his bed. His wife and children were right there and saw it all. They took him outside and held him while someone stabbed him twenty-five times, and then they cut his throat. They threw him high into the air, and each one stamped upon his body before they left.

"There were thirty more about the same time who went to Boudinot's house. They tricked him into walking out with them. They asked him for some medicine. When they were away from the house, they stabbed him in the back and hacked his head with axes. Stand Watie, his brother, has offered ten thousand dollars for the names of the killers."

Nickajack drew a deep breath and sighed heavily.

"This is what I've been afraid would happen," he said.

"That's not all," said Coffee. "There was a third group. They ambushed Major Ridge on the road. He was riding along on his horse, and they shot him from hiding. They shot him five times."

Nickajack sank down heavily on his haunches and leaned back against the house. He stared off into the woods, thinking about the work that had gone into his new home, thinking about his family. The thing he had dreaded was begun. How long would it last? When would it be over? He turned his head slowly, rolling it against the side of the house, his eyes sweeping from the right to the left, and as he did, he noticed on the back of Coffee's horse the shiny new saddle from Eli Johnson's store. He thought about asking Coffee how he had managed to purchase the saddle, but somehow the time just didn't seem right. The question didn't seem very important.

CHAPTER 12

"Gentlemen of the jury," Lynch was saying, "we have seen our own country—and it is our country, even though we are but recently arrived here—we have seen that country become a lawless land, overrun by bandits and murderers. No one is safe. Every day we hear of another atrocity, another brutal and senseless slaying. Our neighbors and ourselves, our wives and children are not safe. Any one of us could be the next victim. Who knows when murderers will burst into our very homes and shoot us down at our dinner tables or drag us from our beds at night to slash at us with knives and hatchets. Murderers run at large and do their evil deeds at will.

"And we are not alone. Do not be lulled into inaction by the promises of the Government of the United States made in the fraudulent treaty which

brought us here. They promised that we would be
secure in our new lands forever, but I promise you,
gentlemen, they are watching. The eyes of the
United States are on us, and if they perceive that we
cannot order our own affairs, if they adjudge that we
cannot control the lawlessness within our own bor-
ders, do not think for a minute that they will not
seize upon that fact for an excuse to once again
encroach upon our rightful sovereign powers. They
wait for us to give them that excuse."

Here the prosecutor paused. He paced away and
then back toward the jury, and then he leaned toward them confidentially.

"Gentlemen," he said, "the defense will speak to
you next, and I imagine that my opponent will try
to make you believe that this case is fraught with
politics. He will tell you that his client is a victim of
the bitter hostilities that have developed in our nation as a result of the recent removal. He will tell
you that Nickajack is not a political man. That he
just happened to remove from the east at the same
time as did the members of the Treaty Party and that
he has been persecuted because of that unfortunate
association. Do not be deceived.

"This trial is not about politics. This is a murder
trial. That man over there, that man called Nickajack, is here because he is guilty of a cold-blooded,
wanton murder. He stood on a public road with a

loaded pistol in his hand and shot to death a fellow citizen, another Cherokee, for no apparent reason, with no known provocation. His sole defense is that his innocent victim was raising a rifle with intent to shoot at him, but two eyewitnesses have sworn in this court that Common Disturber was not armed. Nickajack admits the killing, and in admitting that, he admits that he has also broken another of our laws. The carrying of guns is forbidden. Will you believe a man who boldly defies the law and admits it to our faces, or two reliable witnesses against him?

"You have no recourse but to find this man guilty of murder."

Lynch may have said more, but Nickajack did not hear. His mind had only briefly escaped from the past. He was driving his wagon down the road toward Eli Johnson's store. Coffee Soldier was seated beside him. The white mule was harnessed between the staves. They needed some money for tobacco and coffee and a few other things they could not grow or gather or hunt for themselves. It was late August, and they had loaded the wagon with turnips, onions and corn to sell or barter at Johnson's store. As they neared the store, they could see a horse was tied out front.

"Look," said Nickajack. "It's Spaniard's horse."

Inside they found Spaniard and Johnson seated before the big fireplace drinking coffee and smoking. Johnson got two more chairs and invited Nickajack and Coffee to join them.

"We're talking about the new government," said Spaniard.

"What new government?" asked Coffee.

"John Ross, I bet," said Nickajack.

"You're right," said Spaniard. "It's the old Cherokee Nation come west. They've settled it between the two governments, and John Ross has won."

"We went to a meeting," said Coffee, "but nothing was settled."

"They've had two more since then," said Johnson. "At the first one, they agreed to agree. Actually it was a meeting of Ross's followers with just a few of the Old Settlers present. They adopted a resolution that united the eastern and western Cherokees 'into one body politic under the style and title of the Cherokee Nation.' I suppose it could be said that such a resolution has no meaning since the officials of the Cherokee Nation West took no part in its adoption."

"Of course it's not legal," said Coffee.

"They also said that the murders of the Ridges and Boudinot weren't murders at all, since those men had violated a law that calls for death, and they said that the murderers would be free from prosecution."

"It's not right for them to do that," said Coffee.

"It could be argued either way," said Spaniard. "The Cherokee Nation did have a law against the selling of Cherokee land. Right?"

"Well, yes," said Coffee.

"And the penalty for violating that law was death. Right?"

"That's true," said Nickajack.

"I believe that Major Ridge himself was an executioner at one time for that law," said Spaniard.

"Yes," said Coffee. "I remember that time. Major Ridge helped to kill Doublehead when Doublehead sold some of our land back east. But I don't think it's the same thing."

"It's the same thing," said Johnson. "When something is against the law, it makes no difference *why* someone has broken the law. He just broke it. That's all."

"You mean if Doublehead sold our land to make money for himself, and Major Ridge sold our land to save the People, they are equally guilty?" asked Nickajack.

"That's right," said Johnson. "Under the law, they are equally guilty."

"But what about John Ross dissolving the Cherokee Nation West?" said Coffee. "Is that legal?"

"It's questionable," said Spaniard, "but it doesn't matter. At the second meeting, Old Settlers were there. And they all agreed, and they adopted a new constitution. So now once again, there is one Cherokee Nation."

"And the chief is John Ross," said Coffee.

"The chief is John Ross," said Spaniard, nodding his head in agreement.

Nickajack took a sip of his coffee and put the cup down on the floor. He took his pipe out of his pocket and filled it with tobacco.

"Well," he said, "now maybe everything will be all right."

"Maybe," said Spaniard.

Nickajack leaned forward, reaching into the fireplace for a burning stick to light his pipe. He puffed a few puffs, getting it started and sending up great clouds of blue-gray smoke.

"I don't know," said Coffee. "Maybe not."

*   *   *

"Gentlemen of the jury," said Colonel Walker, standing up and moving toward the jurors, "my client does not deny that he is guilty of the killing of Common Disturber. The defense does not dispute that fact. My client does deny that the killing was a murder.

"Common Disturber and the two men who appeared before you as eyewitnesses, Thomas Fox Elders and Hair Campbell, on the day in question were standing in the public road armed and blocking the path of my client as he rode from the trading post of Eli Johnson back toward his own home. My client's pistol was in his belt. Yes, gentlemen, we are aware of the law against the carrying of firearms in the Cherokee Nation. But Nickajack's home is in the wilderness, away from the comfort and protection of the law. Even so, we stipulate that he is guilty of that infraction. But not of murder. There was some brief discussion. The three men blocking the road refused to move. Then Common Disturber raised his rifle. My client drew out his pistol and fired first, killing Common Disturber in defense of his own life. He then spurred his mule ahead, and the other two men, the men who claim to be mere eyewitnesses, flung their weapons, hand axes and clubs, after my client as he fled for his home.

"That was an act of self-defense. It was not an act of murder. Why were these three men laying in wait for Nickajack, intending to take his life? Previously, they had been among a band of men who rode to the home of Coffee Soldier, a friend and neighbor of my client. We can only assume that these men, men who had suffered the forced migration from the old country, were seeking revenge for their suffering by the deaths of anyone associated with the so-called Treaty Party. Nickajack and Coffee Soldier came west with members of that party. These two men, Nickajack and Coffee Soldier, were not signers of the treaty, gentlemen of the jury. They simply made the move along with those signers. Yet these men seeking revenge, sought out Coffee Soldier because of his association with the Ridges. They rode to his house intending to murder him. Instead, Coffee Soldier, defending his home, his life, his family, slew one of their number, and they fled. Nickajack was there at Coffee Soldier's house on that occasion.

"We therefore assume, gentlemen of the jury, that Common Disturber, Thomas Fox Elders and Hair Campbell had laid an ambush for my client on that fateful day. As was the case at Coffee Soldier's house, their ambush backfired on them, and one of their own instead was killed. Killed, I repeat, in self-defense.

"Gentlemen, this man Nickajack is not a murderer. Even in self-defense he was a reluctant killer. He is a modest, unassuming man. A man of the land. A man with a wife and children. A man just trying to make a new home here in this new nation, just as we all are trying.

"Gentlemen, do not allow politics to color your judgment in this case. This court is an instrument of a government dominated at present by one political party. My client, though he himself is not a political man, has been associated with a minority party in opposition to the party in control. Do not allow the political situation to make a sham of justice. Render a just and true verdict. Find my client Nickajack not guilty of the murder of Common Disturber. In so doing you will show the world that the Cherokee Nation is a capable and civilized nation, a nation of laws, with a functioning court system that dispenses justice for all fairly and equally.

"I thank you."

CHAPTER 13

The hopes for peace that Nickajack had expressed in his conversation at Johnson's store with Johnson, Coffee and Spanish Jack had proved to be false hopes. There was no peace. The killings continued. It had not ended with the deaths of the three leaders of the Treaty Party. Twenty-one men had signed the Treaty of New Echota, and those who had suffered over the Trail of Tears as a result had lost maybe four thousand friends and relatives along the way. They were not satisfied with the three assassinations. And even if the avengers had been satisfied with the three deaths, the friends and relatives of the Ridges and Boudinot were incensed and now they wanted revenge. There was news of at least one new killing almost every day. It seemed as if a civil war was brewing inside the Cherokee Nation. The new land was being baptized in the blood of Cherokees.

Nickajack tried to stay at home. At Johnson's store all the talk was of politics and of the killings. And it was getting that way with Coffee. Sometimes Nickajack wondered what he and Coffee had talked about all those years before they had this trouble. When he was visiting with Coffee, he looked for opportunities to change the subject, to talk of the old days or of work to be done, of the weather, of anything besides the killings and the politics. Sometimes it worked, and sometimes it did not. And so Nickajack's visits to Coffee became less frequent, and when Coffee stopped by to visit Nickajack, Nickajack tried to find work to do around his home. Usually Coffee would help him, but sometimes even then he talked. And even then the talk was of the kind that Nickajack did not want to hear.

"But you can't ignore it, my friend," Coffee said to him one day. "It's all around us. Our friends are being killed. It's like a war right here in our country, and our children and grandchildren must grow up here. We have to know what's going on around us, and we have to help to find a way to stop it, to make this country safe for our families."

"I'm not a part of it," said Nickajack. "I didn't sign the treaty. I don't belong to any party."

These discussions never really concluded. They simply stopped abruptly when one or the other man realized he was about to become angry. Then he would change the subject quickly with a remark, usually about the weather, and soon after that, the one who was the visitor would make his excuse and go home. It was during this tense period that Spanish Jack stopped by again. He was accompanied by another Indian on horseback, a large and jovial full-blood.

" 'Siyo, Nikutsegi," said Spanish Jack. "This is my friend Blackcoat."

"Then he is also my friend," said Nickajack. "Climb down and rest yourselves."

The two riders dismounted, and Nickajack shook their hands.

"We'll have something to eat," he said, "and then we'll talk."

They ate, and then they sat on chairs outside. They had cups of coffee, and they smoked their pipes.

"How is your neighbor these days?" asked Spaniard.

"Coffee?" said Nickajack.

"Yes," said Spaniard. "How is Coffee?"

"He's well," said Nickajack. "I don't see so much of him as I used to."

"Oh?" said Spaniard. "Is something wrong?"

"No," said Nickajack. "I'm just so busy."

He puffed at his pipe, contemplating his lie.

"We always talk of politics and all the killing," he said. "It's not the way it used to be."

"Nothing ever is," said Spaniard. "Things

change. We all change. The world changes. And yet, they say that time is a circle, and we all return to the same place we began."

"So maybe things only seem to change," said Nickajack.

"Or maybe," said Blackcoat, "things change for a little while. Then they change back to what they were before."

Spanish Jack puffed his pipe and stared off toward the north. Suddenly he seemed distant and cold.

"The past is always with us," he said. "No matter what some people try to tell us, the past is always here."

Nickajack stood up and stretched. He paced away from Spaniard and Blackcoat a few yards. When he spoke his back was turned on them.

"Maybe I'm the one who is wrong about all this," he said. "Coffee says that it's our country, and we have to be concerned. But I don't belong to any parties. I didn't sign any treaty. I'm not a politician. I don't even understand politics and treaties, and I don't want to be bothered with this fight."

"You're not wrong," said Spaniard. "It's not my fight either. My fight is somewhere else."

*   *   *

Spanish Jack and Blackcoat stayed the night, and in the morning they rode north. Nickajack thought that he knew where Spaniard was going. He knew what kind of business Spaniard was about, and he knew what Spanish Jack considered to be his fight. It was supposed to be over, but Spanish Jack had said that the past is always with us. Well, Nickajack wanted no part of Spaniard's fight, just as he wanted no part of the fight between the Ross Party and the Treaty Party.

Several days passed uneventfully, and Nickajack could almost believe that he was finally being left alone. He worked around his farm. He played with his children, and he made love to his wife. He did not, however, visit with Coffee. That was the one reminder he had that all was not well, for had everything been well, he would certainly have taken some time to visit with his best friend. Two weeks after the visit of Spanish Jack and Blackcoat, Nickajack found that he had to make a trip to Johnson's store.

"Have you heard about Jack Spaniard?" said Johnson.

"I saw him ten days ago or so," said Nickajack. "He was going north, and he stopped at my house for the night. He had a friend with him, a man named Blackcoat."

"Blackcoat came by here," said Johnson. "Day before yesterday, I think. Yeah. That was it. Day before yesterday. But he was by himself."

"Where was Spanish Jack?"

"The Spaniard is lost," said Johnson. "That's

what Blackcoat said. They rode up into the Osage country, hoping for the opportunity to commit some mischief on that nation of liars. Jack liked to steal their horses, you know. And he turned his pleasure into profit. He sold the horses in Choctaw country, sometimes even down to Texas."

"Spanish Jack is a horsethief?" said Nickajack.

"Well, it ain't like stealing in your own country, now is it? Not when you're stealing from the Osage."

Johnson was speaking English, and Nickajack was speaking Cherokee. Each could understand the other. Nickajack wondered why Johnson had decided to use English on this occasion. Perhaps because of the subject matter of the conversation. He couldn't be sure.

"At any rate," said Johnson, "they rode on up into the Osage country looking for likely horses, and knowing Jack, I imagine that he was kind of looking for Osages, too. Not just keeping his eyes open for his own good, I mean, but really looking for some to do them harm. You know?"

"Yes," said Nickajack. "I think so."

"They'd made three camps or four, Blackcoat told me," said Johnson, "and on that fourth day, he could tell that they were being watched. He looked at Spanish Jack, he said, and Jack looked at him, and neither of them said a word. But they both knew. Still they rode north, and Blackcoat begun to get nervous. Stealing a few horses to make a few dollars had seemed like a pretty good idea to him, but he hadn't counted on Jack's obsession with the Osages.

" 'There are more of them now,' he said to Jack.

" 'I know,' said Jack. That's all he said. 'I know.'

"They rode on for a spell, and Blackcoat held his tongue, but the hair was standing out on the back of his neck. He sensed that they was gathering around them in the hills and up ahead. Finally he spoke up.

" 'Jack,' he said, 'they're all around us now, and I think they're waiting to ambush us up there.'

" 'Of course they are,' said Spanish Jack. 'They're like a pack of wolves. They're cowards. That's the only way they know to fight.'

"Jack rode on straight ahead. He was sitting tall in his saddle, holding that long rifle across his chest, two loaded pistols stuck in his sash. Up ahead of them, the road took a sharp curve, but straight ahead, off the road, three Osages rode into sight and just sat there waiting. Jack rode straight toward them never changing his pace. Blackcoat slowed his horse.

" 'Jack,' he said, his voice low, 'turn back.'

" '*Do na da go huh,*' said Jack. 'We shall see one another again,' and he didn't even look back. He just kept riding. Blackcoat stopped. He waited, and he watched as Jack rode closer to the three Osages up on the rise. Finally, close enough for an easy rifle shot, Jack stopped.

" *Je m'appelle Jacques L'Espagnol,* ' he shouted, and he raised his long rifle and fired. The Osage in the middle dropped from his horse, and the other two shouted and kicked their horses in the sides and rode straight for Jack. Blackcoat thought for an instant about racing ahead and joining in the fight, but four more Osages appeared on the horizon. Blackcoat held back. He told me that he was no coward, but he said that it was almost as if Spanish Jack was on a suicide mission, and he had no intention of joining in on that sort of thing. Jack charged the Osages, tossing aside his rifle and pulling out his pistols. The two Osages were already charging at Jack, and as they rode past each other, Jack shot one off his horse. He fired his second pistol at the other one, but he missed the shot. The four on the horizon scattered as Jack rode into their midst. Up on the edge, he turned his horse, tossed aside his empty pistols and pulled out his belt ax.

" 'Come on,' he shouted at them, still talking to them in French. 'You're the shit of mangy dogs.'

"Then one rode straight toward him, and Spanish Jack split his skull with one stroke of his ax. He dismounted quickly then and reached into his saddlebags where he had two more pistols stashed. He dropped another Osage with one shot, and his horse ran off a ways. And as he raised the second pistol to take aim, one let fly an arrow from some distance away. The shaft buried itself in the breast of Spanish

Jack, and he staggered back a step or so with the impact of it. Blackcoat hadn't noticed until that moment, but the horizon upon which Jack was standing must have been the edge of a precipice, for when he staggered back, he fell. The Osages swarmed around the spot, and at least a couple of them slipped over the edge to go down and finish the job. That was all that Blackcoat saw, for it was then that he turned and fled. I fear we'll never see our Spanish Jack again."

"I will miss him," said Nickajack.

"So will we all," said Johnson, now speaking in Cherokee. "But out of every ill comes good, and this at last will probably bring peace with the Osages. Jack was the last hold out. He just wouldn't quit."

"Why did he hate the Osages so much?" asked Nickajack.

"Years ago," said Johnson, "when the war between the Osage and the western Cherokees was in full swing, they killed his wife and stole his children. The children have never been located. They're probably dead. Or maybe—"

Johnson paused, a curious expression on his leathery old face.

"Or what?" asked Nickajack.

"Or worse yet," said Johnson. "Funny I never thought of it before. They might have grown up Osage. It could be Jack's own son that killed him, and no one ever the wiser."

*   *   *

It had been some time since Nickajack had visited
with Coffee Soldier, and he thought that the news
regarding the fate of Spanish Jack was a good excuse.
So he went to Coffee's house. Coffee was out near
the road stacking rocks, presumably clearing them
away to make another field for plowing. Nickajack
reined in his mule and slipped down off its back.

"'Siyo," said Coffee.

"'Siyo, Kawi," said Nickajack. "You're working
hard."

"I want to plant some corn out here," said Coffee.

"That's good," said Nickajack. He picked up
some rocks and threw them on the stack that Coffee
had started. "I just came from Johnson's store."

"Ah," said Coffee. "Did Eli tell you tales?"

"He told me about Spanish Jack. The Osages
have killed him."

Coffee stopped working. He sat down on his rock
pile, breathing hard from his labor.

"That's too bad," he said. "I liked him."

"Yes," said Nickajack. "I liked him too. But
maybe it's for the best after all. Johnson says that
now our troubles with the Osages will probably be
over."

Coffee thought for a moment in silence.

"Yes," he said. "That part is good. We have enough troubles now among ourselves."

Nickajack did not want to talk about the internal strife in the Cherokee Nation. That was the very reason he had not seen Coffee for some time. Why must Coffee always find a way to turn the conversation back to politics and the killings? But it wasn't just Coffee. It was almost everyone, everyone except Nickajack. He wondered if there was something wrong with him that he was the only Cherokee who didn't want to talk about those things. He wondered if there were others like him somewhere. He bent to pick up a rock and toss it toward the pile on which Coffee was still sitting.

"John Ross is to blame for all this trouble," said Coffee. He stood and paced out in the field. He picked up a rock and threw it at the pile. "He and his followers intend to kill off all the Treaty Party. All of us."

Nickajack wasn't at all sure that John Ross was really to blame for all their troubles. If anyone was to blame, he thought, it seemed more likely that the Government of the United States was the one. But it was too big and too remote to attack. People needed something near at hand to blame. So Coffee and the Treaty Party blamed John Ross. John Ross and his party blamed the Treaty Party. And they were killing each other. It seemed to Nickajack as if everyone had gone crazy.

"The world is out of balance," he said. "Someone has done something bad. Or failed to do something. I don't know."

"Are you thinking that Major Ridge and the others who signed the treaty are the ones who threw things out of balance?" said Coffee.

Nickajack could see that the conversation could easily develop into an argument. He did not want to argue with his best friend about politics. He did not even want to be thinking about politics.

"I don't know," he said again. "I think that I had better go on home."

Nickajack headed for his mule, grazing patiently along the side of the road. Somewhere in the distance a blue jay shouted.

"Wait a minute," said Coffee. Nickajack stopped. He turned back to face Coffee.

"I'm going to kill a hog in the morning," said Coffee. "Bring your family, and we'll all eat fresh meat."

Nickajack nodded in agreement. It was good. Old friends should not part on the verge of anger.

"All right," he said. "Tomorrow we'll all come. We'll come early to help."

"I'll be at work before you get here," said Coffee. "Maybe I'll have all the work done."

"Maybe you won't be out of bed yet," said Nickajack. He climbed up on the back of the white mule and headed for home.

CHAPTER 14

Nickajack had taken his family to Coffee's house early the next morning. He knew that there was lots of work to do, and Coffee and his family would be glad to have all the help they could get. They arrived just after sunup, and it was obvious that Coffee and his family had already been busy for a while. The fires were going. One large black kettle of water was on to boil. Nickajack unloaded the black kettle he had brought from his house, and they filled it with water and set it on a fire. Coffee had driven the hog into a pen the night before. Everything was ready.

They killed, skinned and butchered the hog. It was a messy, all day job, and everyone worked, even the children. Most of the meat they salted and put away, but they saved out enough fresh meat for a big meal for everyone at the end of the long workday. They were all exhausted from the hard work, and the meal was delicious. Nickajack felt good. He had spent a day working with his best friend, with both their families. They had shared work and fellowship and food, and they had not talked about politics or about the unrest which swirled around them. It was late afternoon or early evening. The day was almost done. It was almost like old times, Nickajack thought. Maybe after all it could be that way again. But then it happened. Coffee leaned back in his chair and sighed.

"This has been a good day," he said.

"Yes," said Nickajack. "This is the way it should be."

"It would be like this all the time," said Coffee, "if John Ross and his followers would come to their senses. They've brought so much trouble here with them that the peace of people's homes is disturbed."

Nickajack felt his jaws tighten. He did not want the day to end like this. He did not want the conversation to go any further. And then he got his wish, but in a totally unexpected and unwelcome way. That was when Archie Drownding and the other men had ridden up to Coffee Soldier's house.

*   *   *

"You've heard all the evidence," Judge Spears was saying to the jury. "Now it's up to you to render a verdict according to law. If you have any personal feelings on this matter, you must set them aside. You must set aside clan and family issues and political alliances. You have heard the defendant's claim that three men waylaid him along a public road, all of them being armed, and threatened his life, and that he shot Common Disturber in self-defense. You have also heard the testimony of two eyewitnesses to the slaying of Common Disturber. Both of them swear that the defendant Nickajack shot Common Disturber, not in self-defense, but for no apparent reason, deliberately, and that at the time Common Disturber was unarmed. The defendant admits that he was armed and admits the shooting. You must decide which story to believe. You must determine whether Nickajack acted in self-defense or committed cold-blooded murder.

"I cannot emphasize enough to you the importance of maintaining law and order in our nation. The United States, perhaps the world, is watching the Cherokee Nation carefully to see whether or not we can maintain a civilized society. They know about the murders that have taken place. They know about our civil unrest. Will they also know that we allow that violence to go unchecked, murderers to go unpunished? If you determine that a murder was committed, it is your duty to declare it by rendering a verdict of guilty."

Nickajack watched as the Catchers at the door escorted the jury out of the courtroom. He felt a blast of cold air when the door was opened. The judge then called two more Catchers to escort Nickajack back to Smith's to wait for the jury to complete its deliberations. Colonel Walker went with Nickajack. Soon they were seated by the fire at Smith's place, and Mrs. Smith gave them each a bowl of stew and a cup of coffee. They ate in silence.

"I, uh, I don't know," said Colonel Walker, "what the jury will say, but—"

"I know," said Nickajack.

The jury was not out for long, and soon the court was reconvened. Spears rapped his gavel on the table and called the court to order.

"Has the jury reached a verdict?" he said.

One man stood up.

"Yes, we have, Your Honor," he said.

"Read the verdict," said Spears.

"We find the defendant Nickajack guilty of the murder of Common Disturber."

Walker expelled the breath he had been holding and leaned his head forward heavily in his hands, his elbows resting on the table. Nickajack gave no sign of having heard or understood.

"There is no need to postpone sentencing," said Spears. "Our law is clear. Nickajack, you have been found guilty of the willful murder of a fellow citizen, and for that act, I have no choice except to sentence you to hang by the neck until you are dead. Sentence will be carried out five days from today. In the meantime you will be held in the custody of the Lighthorse Police. This court is adjourned."

The Catchers came for Nickajack, and as he stood to be lead away, Colonel Walker spoke to him rapidly.

"This is not necessarily the last word," he said. "There is an appeal to the Principal Chief possible under the law. You'll be hearing from me."

"Thank you," said Nickajack.

Colonel Walker turned to one of the Catchers.

"Will he be at Smith's?" he said.

"Yes," said the Catcher.

Before they got to the door with Nickajack, Coffee Soldier caught them. Nickajack was puzzled for a moment. Had he known that Coffee was there? He must have known. Coffee was there with his family and with Nickajack's family. Nickajack's mind had been playing him so many tricks that he couldn't remember, couldn't be sure, whether or not his family and friends should be there just at that moment.

"Can I go with you?" he said. "I and my family? We're here with his family. We'd all like to be with him now."

The Catchers looked at each other. Then one of them answered Coffee.

"You can come along," he said. "But not everyone can come in at once."

"Thank you," said Coffee, and Coffee and both families started to follow Nickajack and the Catchers out the door. Colonel Walker overheard, and he followed them too. He caught up with Coffee and walked along beside him.

"Coffee," he said. "You're Nickajack's best friend."

"That's right," said Coffee.

"You've known him all your life?"

"Yes."

"I'm going to prepare a petition to the Chief," said Walker. "I want you to sign it first. Will you?"

"Of course I will," said Coffee. "Do you think the Chief will let him go?"

"I don't know," said Walker, "but it's the only thing left. We have to try it."

"I'll sign it," said Coffee, "and I know some other ones who will."

"I'll see you again before the end of the day," said Walker.

*   *   *

Nickajack sat again in the chair by the fire in Smith's house. The two Catchers stood at the door. Nickajack's family and Coffee and his family were gathered around. Nickajack sat in silence. What does a dead man say to his family and friends? At last Colonel Walker returned with his newly written petition asking the Principal Chief to review the case. Coffee Soldier wrote his name, and Cabin

Smith wrote his. Coffee gave Walker a list of names of people to see.

"They'll all sign," he said.

"I'll find as many of them as I can," said Walker. He turned to Nickajack. "It may take a day or two to get the signatures, but I'll be back. We have five days."

Nickajack nodded his head slowly, and Colonel Walker headed for the door. He was about to go out when one of the Catchers spoke to him.

"Can I sign your paper?" he said.

"Why, of course," said Colonel Walker.

"Me too," said the other one. And both the Catchers signed. Colonel Walker left to find more signers. After a long and uncomfortable silence, Nickajack spoke.

"There is nothing more that you can do here," he said. "All of you. You've been away from home too long already. Coffee, take them home. Your family and mine."

They protested, of course, but in the end, Nickajack prevailed. They left.

*   *   *

He dreamed that night. He dreamed of death. He saw himself, a walking ghost. He stood apart and looked at his own body dangling from a rope. He saw again the death of Archie Drownding, and once again he killed Common Disturber. He saw Spanish Jack kill the Osages once more and take their scalps. There was blood everywhere, blood on the ground where he was walking, blood on his hands. And he saw Spanish Jack fall over the edge of a high mountain ridge, an arrow in his breast. And he saw the face of death.

*   *   *

The next day Nickajack sat still and somber beside the fire. He ate when food was given to him, and he drank coffee when it was offered. He asked for nothing. He did not speak except when he was spoken to, and then he answered questions as briefly as possible. Colonel Walker did not return. No one came to visit. That night he dreamed again of the images of death.

*   *   *

The second day was much like the first, but the dreams that night were no longer of violence and blood. Instead he walked throughout the night, a shadow. No one saw him. No one could hear him speak. The third day Colonel Walker came back. He walked in with the look of defeat about him, but Nickajack was not surprised. He was not disappointed. He was well beyond that, for he was already walking in the Darkening Land, the land where spirits go.

"Nickajack," said Colonel Walker, "you have lots of friends. I got all the names I needed, and I took the petition to the Chief. He read it while I waited. He thought over the paper for a long while before he spoke to me.

" 'I cannot reverse the decision of the court in a case like this,' he said. 'I can delay the sentence, though. Show up in court with your client on the appointed day for execution.' That's all he said."

* * *

They were walking from Smith's house to the small building which served as the courtroom when Coffee Soldier came running toward them.

"Colonel Walker," he said. "Where are you going?"

"We're going back to the court," said the Colonel. "The Chief read my petition and delayed the sentence."

"Nickajack won't hang?" said Coffee.

"He won't hang today," said Walker. "That's all we know for now."

"Can I go with you to the court?"

"Of course," said Walker.

Coffee fell in step beside Nickajack. Nickajack did not speak.

"There's hope," said Coffee.

*   *   *

The judge banged down his gavel and called the court to order. Then he sat for a moment and stared at some papers there before him on the table. At last he spoke.

"Nickajack," he said, "today you were to hang. Instead you're back here in my court. You are here because your attorney carried a petition to the Chief on your behalf. That is your right and privilege under the law. The Principal Chief called me for a conference. He said that he would not consider reversing the order of this court. The guilty verdict stands. He did not see here any miscarriage of justice. He was, however, moved by the plight of your family, your innocent wife and children. Why, he asked, should they suffer for what you have done? Why should we make more victims? Our joint decision in conference was this. You have been sentenced in a court of law to hang for the crime of willful murder, and hang you shall. You will be released on your own recognizance to return to your wife and family in order that you may do all you can to prepare them for the life ahead, provided that you promise me today that you'll return to Tahlequah in just one year, that's one year from today, to keep your appointment with the executioner. Mr. Walker, does your client understand?"

Walker spoke to Nickajack in Cherokee to make sure that he had understood. A brief conversation followed, and Walker faced the judge again.

"He understands, Your Honor, and he gives his word."

*   *   *

Everyone left the courtroom but Nickajack and Coffee and Colonel Walker. They sat for a while in silence, not even looking at one another. At last Walker spoke.

"I'm sorry," he said. "There is no further appeal under the law."

"You did everything you could do, Colonel Walker," said Nickajack. "It's all right."

"So," said Coffee. "You have one year."

Before leaving the courtroom, Judge Spears had given some paper to Colonel Walker. Walker handed it to Nickajack.

"Do you understand this calendar?" he said.

"No," said Nickajack. "What is it?"

"Each one of these squares is a day," said Walker. "This one is today."

He flipped several pages and pointed to another square, which he drew a circle around.

"This is the day you are to return."

He turned back to the first page again and pointed again to the first square.

"This is today," he repeated. "Each day you can mark off one square. Like this." He drew a line through the number in the square. "When you have marked off all the days before the one I circled, you'll know it's time."

"I see," said Nickajack, and he took the calendar and the marking stick the Colonel offered him and tucked them in a pocket.

"I'll bring your mule," said Coffee, and he left the room. Nickajack felt the cold from outside come rushing in while the door was opened.

"Nickajack," said Colonel Walker, "I think the Chief would have liked to let you go. I think he knows that the trial wasn't fair. Oh, I know it was Ross people on the jury, and the judge is a Ross man, but I think John Ross wants to be fair. He just couldn't go against his own court. Our court really. And he couldn't risk offending his own supporters. I think that, at the same time, he thought that giving you a year's time before the sentence is to be carried out was a way of showing a little leniency and, perhaps, a way of trying to appease some of the opposition party."

"Politics?" said Nickajack.

"Yes," said Walker. "I'm afraid so. I'm afraid that it was politics from the beginning to the end. It shouldn't be like that, but it is."

"I never liked politics," said Nickajack. "Now I

know why. I tried to stay away from politics, but I couldn't, and it has killed me."

*   *   *

He went outside and stood in the cold. Colonel Walker said good-by and left him there. He could see Coffee coming, riding his horse and leading the white mule, and the cold began to penetrate his body. It was not bitter cold outside. He had suffered worse cold. It was not that the cold was so intense. It was just that it was moving inside him, and then it was almost as if the cold that he was feeling was coming *from* inside, and he knew that he would carry it with him wherever he went. Coffee rode up and stopped beside him, and Nickajack pulled himself up onto the mule's back.

"*Wado,*" he said. "*Inena.*"

They rode in silence out of Tahlequah and turned east toward the river.

CHAPTER 15

When Nickajack left the courtroom, he was a ghost. In his mind he was dead already. He was a ghost who had been granted a year on earth to deal with certain obligations. But he was a ghost. He almost thought that he was invisible. He almost felt like he could walk through trees and walls and rocks. He felt permeated by a clammy numbness, but it was not the December air that caused him to feel that way. It was death. Colonel Walker had said that he would appeal the case as far as he could. There was a process provided for in the constitution, and he would pursue it to the end. Well, he had reached the end. Nickajack thanked the Colonel for his concern and for all his work. He did not tell the lawyer to forget it, but he knew that it would all be to no avail. He was already a ghost.

Coffee Soldier rode home with Nickajack. It was

a solemn ride and a quiet one. Nickajack had nothing to say, had no desire to speak, for he was dead. Coffee wanted to talk to his friend, but he could think of nothing appropriate, nothing fitting to the occasion. They stopped at the river, and Coffee studied the ford.

"I think we can still cross easily here," he said. "The water is low."

They nudged their mounts forward and splashed through the icy waters. When they came out on the other side, Nickajack spoke. Coffee thought that the voice sounded faraway, and it sent a chill up his spine.

"Will you look after my family when I'm gone?" he said.

"Of course I will," said Coffee. "I'll think of them the same as I do my own family. Don't worry about that."

"Thank you," said Nickajack. They rode on for a while in silence.

"Coffee," said Nickajack, "my wife is young and pretty. My children are good children."

"Yes," said Coffee. "That's true."

"Lots of men have two wives," said Nickajack. "Some have more than two."

"Yes, they do," said Coffee. "If they are rich enough to take care of them."

"My place and yours together could almost make a man rich," said Nickajack. "Do you think so?"

"Maybe," said Coffee. "They're both good places. We've both worked hard on them."

"You have only one wife," said Nickajack.

*   *   *

At home Nickajack was quiet and methodical. He told his wife what had happened, but he did not say much more. She soon realized that he would say almost nothing that was not necessary. He ate little. He slept beside her in their bed, but she never saw him sleep. She saw him lying there on his back staring straight up at the ceiling. He was still like that when she had fallen asleep, and when she woke up in the morning, he was already up and dressed and working. When the children tried to speak to him, he touched their heads and looked at them with sad eyes. Then he went on with his work.

The first morning after his return home from the trial and the sentencing, Nickajack sat at the table and laid out his calendar. He took the marking stick and drew an X through a number just the way that Colonel Walker had done. He did not know what the number said. He could not read letters or numbers, but he remembered that Colonel Walker had said that each box was a day. He would mark off each day and keep track of the passing of time. He turned the pages of the calendar until he reached the last page, and he looked at the number in the square that Colonel Walker had circled. "This is the day for you to be back here in Tahlequah," Walker had said. Nickajack's wife walked up to look over his shoulder. She had seen him mark out the number in the square.

"What is that?" she said.

"These are my days that the judge gave me," he answered. He put the papers and the marking stick away. Each day after that, the first thing that Nickajack did in the morning after getting out of bed and dressing was to mark a day off his calendar. Then he went to work. The winter work had already begun before he went to trial. It had been interrupted forcibly for a period of time, but now he resumed it. He cut firewood every day. Always there would be more need for firewood. So each day he cut and stacked. Each day the stack grew. If he had been alive, he would have enjoyed the work. It was routine and required little if any thought. He cut and he stacked.

He took down his harness for the white mule, and he scraped it and cleaned it. Then he rubbed it with tallow and hung it up on a peg high up out of the reach of mice. He killed a hog and butchered it and smoked the meat. He uncovered the potatoes he had buried last September and checked them over carefully. A few were showing signs of rot. He took them out and threw them away. The wandering hogs would find them. Then he re-covered the rest of the potatoes for safe keeping. He did the same for his onions and his turnips. He checked the house for cracks and leaks, chinking them when he found them, using old clothes sometimes and sometimes mud.

In the bony month which the whites called February, when the hardest part of winter was done, but when it was still cold enough to kill the exposed roots of upturned grass and the worms and beetles that were snug beneath the ground, he plowed his garden. He cleaned out the mule's shed, taking the old straw and droppings out to spread the rich and smelly mixture over the freshly upturned ground. He cut more wood. It was all routine, all motion of habit. He worked like a machine even though he had never watched a machine work.

In early March he hitched the white mule to his two-stave wagon and drove it to the middle of the creek nearby. He gave it a thorough washing, then drove it back to the house. He put the mule away, got out his few tools and took apart the wagon, piece by piece. He cleaned each part, made some repairs, greased it and put it back together, good as new, maybe better. He would have taken pride in his work had he been alive. Later that same month he began to plant. He went into the woods and dug some sassafras root from which his wife made tea. The whole family drank the tea to thin their blood for the coming summer. He took a turkey feather and carefully sliced the end to make a sharp quill with which he pierced a large vein in the white mule's neck. He drew out perhaps a half a quart of blood. The mule's system would make new blood and thereby be regenerated.

In May he planted sorghum cane and corn, and in the summer months he began to harvest.

"Don't let the July rains fall on your onions," he said to his children, for there were things that they must know when he was gone. He dug up onions and potatoes and turnips. He tied the onions and hung them up from the eaves of the house. He piled potatoes in the shade of a large oak tree. In September he harvested his corn and shocked the stalks. In November he buried his onions, and he started cutting firewood again to replenish the supply for the winter ahead. And it was in November that he climbed on the back of the white mule and rode to see his friend Coffee Soldier.

The meeting was awkward for one between old friends. But the day was warm. Winter had not yet descended. They sat outside with coffee in their cups beside the fire that had cooked Soldier's breakfast. They sat a while in silence.

"It's been a long time since I've seen you," said Coffee Soldier.

"There has been much work to do," said Nickajack. "My days are almost gone."

There was another long and awkward silence.

Each man sipped his coffee and stared off toward the woods. At last Coffee broke the silence.

"My friend," he said, "has anyone been watching you?"

"Who would watch me?" said Nickajack.

"I mean the Catchers," said Coffee. "Have they been around?"

"No," said Nickajack. "Why would they be around to watch me?"

"If no one is watching you," said Coffee, "then you could run away and hide. You don't have to go back—to Tahlequah."

Nickajack's face registered surprise, almost astonishment. Such a thought had not occurred to him before.

"Where would I go?" he said.

"I don't know," said Coffee. "Anyplace. Someplace away from here."

"To live with white men? Or Osages? I don't talk their language. I don't understand their ways. And besides all that, they might not want me there among them. I'm a Cherokee, and I don't know how to live with anyone else."

"You could learn," said Coffee. "You'd live."

"No," said Nickajack. "I told them I would come back."

Riding slowly home on the white mule, Nickajack thought about what Coffee had said. It was true that no one was watching him. It would be easy to run away and hide rather than to show up back at Tahlequah on the appointed day. He wondered for a moment if it was strange that he had not thought of that possibility on his own. To run away. To be a fugitive. To live he knew not where. He had heard of fugitives, of course, of wandering, homeless men who were always hiding their trails, always looking back. And he had always thought of those men as pitiful, wretched creatures, lost souls roaming aimlessly over the face of the earth. He could not imagine a worse kind of life.

Or to run far away, beyond the reach of the Catchers of the Cherokee Nation? To find a place where he could settle down again, not running, not hiding, not watching for the Catchers all the time? He could not begin to imagine such a place. He knew that there was space out there where other people lived. But there would be people, and they would not be his people. He would not know how to live among those people, and he knew that if they were white people, they would be opposed to his presence there among them, just like those in Georgia. It seemed to Nickajack that for a Cherokee there was no place to live except among the Cherokees. For Cherokees the world was small. To go away from where the Cherokees lived would be like leaving the world.

He had been uprooted once, had left the only home he'd ever known, but he had made that move with a larger group. The entire Cherokee Nation was moving. It had been traumatic, but he had not left his world. His world had moved and carried him along. This other kind of move, to run away alone, did not seem to Nickajack even to be a thing within the realm of possibilities. It was not even something to consider. It was a thing only for fantasies and nightmares.

As he rode along he noticed dark clouds moving in, and he thought that he could feel a drop in temperature. It wouldn't be long before the winter came. He was glad that he would be ready for it. He had been noticing signs that made him think the coming winter would be harder and colder than had been the last. The house was well chinked, and he had laid up plenty of firewood. His family would be all right. He wondered if his wife would become Coffee Soldier's second wife. He had hinted to them both that it would probably be a good idea. Maybe they would take the hint. Of course, he thought, he would never know.

Maybe Coffee wouldn't want his wife. He knew that Coffee didn't want him to go back to Tahlequah. Coffee had said, "You don't have to go back . . ." He wondered why he and Coffee did not feel the same way. Coffee had asked if the

Catchers were watching. And they were not. Why were the Catchers not watching him? Because he had told them that he would return on the appointed day, and they had taken him at his word. They had believed him. They had trusted him. Because of that alone, he thought, he should go back. One does not betray a trust. One does not break one's word. For a favor, one must return a favor, and they had given him this year. To run away, to not show up on time, would violate all of his beliefs. It would be rude, discourteous. It would be dishonorable. Why must he go back? He had said that he'd go back.

The thinking was too much, so he drove it from his mind with one last thought. And he realized with some degree of satisfaction that this final thought was in fact the real reason that he must go back to Tahlequah. It was the first reason, and it was the overriding reason. It was the real reason, and it encompassed all the other reasons. He had existed with it for a year almost, had felt its presence every day, and it had become so overwhelming, so much a part of him that he had ceased to think about it, had not thought about it just now until the last. And this was it. He was already dead. He was a ghost walking upon this earth for one last year. He had known it since the day the judge had passed his sentence. It had descended on him like a pall. It had perhaps been true even earlier than that, perhaps since the day of the shooting, the day he killed another man, a Cherokee. He had felt something then, but only when he heard the sentence read in the courtroom had he been able to give it words. He was a walking dead man. He was a ghost, and his time was almost up.

CHAPTER 16

He was so cold that he had stopped feeling cold. He had stopped feeling anything but numb—numb and sick. Deep inside he felt sick, and it was a deathly sickness he felt. Still he moved forward. Still his legs jerked with each step, and when he shivered from the cold, it was with violent spasms that wrenched his whole body. He fell again, and again he considered lying down to rest, but if he did he knew he'd die. He had to keep moving. Some mysterious, fanatical stubbornness drove him on. An unseen and unrelenting force propelled him toward his destination. He would make it. He must make it. And he would make it alone. He had insisted that his wife and children remain at home. They did not need to be subjected to the spectacle that awaited him, and he did not need their presence. Coffee had wanted to accompany him on this final journey as well. Nickajack had told him the same thing he had told his family. Yet he had been afraid that Coffee would come anyway, so he had left early. If Coffee came to go with him, Coffee would not find him at home. He would be too late. Nickajack had said his farewells. He was done with this world. He had just one last appointment to keep.

The wind seemed to intensify, and the ice blew harder against his face. If only he had not lost his seat on the mule while crossing the river, he thought, he would have been all right. But he had gotten soaked in the icy water, and he was freezing, slowly freezing to death. He was in a race with the freezing, he knew. He had to get to shelter and a fire soon, and the nearest shelter was in Tahlequah. There was no way to shorten the trip, no resting place along the way. At last the ground beneath his feet was level. He was no longer walking uphill on the ice. He had reached the top of the rise. Soon he would face a gradual downhill grade, and then he would be there. He walked on.

He was worried about his family, but there was no more he could do. Coffee Soldier had promised to look after them, and Nickajack had done all he could to prepare them for their future. He hoped that his wife would become the second wife of Coffee Soldier. Such things were customary among the Cherokees, although the white missionaries had done their best to discourage the practice. Nickajack thought, though, that it would certainly be preferable to her trying to raise their children alone, and he couldn't think of any other man she might marry. Of course, she might surprise him and find one on her own, one that he had not even thought about. He wondered what kind of life his children would have to look forward to. Would the killing still be going on when they were grown? He hoped not. Perhaps what he was doing would finally put a stop to it. When they had done with him, would they think that had been enough? He hoped so.

Suddenly the ground was sloping downward, and his feet flew out from under him. He landed hard on his backside and slid for a few feet. He managed to stand up again. He thought that he would have to watch more carefully where he put his feet down, but the way his legs were jerking with the cold, he had but little control over where he stepped anyway. He moved ahead, slipping, sliding, falling.

At the bottom of the hill, Nickajack turned south with the road. Tahlequah was just ahead. He could not see the roof of the big council shed for the raging storm, but he knew that it was there. His legs jerked him forward. Each breath was painful. The icy air stabbed at his already frozen lungs. He had a flash of horror that told him he would die there within sight of his goal, but he did not. Someone appeared and hands took hold of him, helping him to stand, turning him and pushing him until he was inside. And it was warm.

He was inside one of the public taverns which stood just outside the capital square. Several people were there. A fire roared in a big fireplace, and they had moved him up close where he could feel the heat. Someone brought a blanket, and someone else pushed up a chair, but he could not sit down. Someone spoke in Cherokee saying that he should get out of his wet clothing, and someone held the blanket up around him, and somehow, with someone's help, he was undressed and wrapped in the blanket. He could feel the warmth from the flames, yet he was still cold. He thought that he would be cold at least until he died. Parts of his body felt as if they would break off at a touch. But at last the convulsive shivers ceased, and at last his joints loosened so that he could sit. Someone asked his name, and he tried to answer, but he could not speak. Someone else said, "Give him more time," and yet another brought him a cup of hot coffee. After he had managed a few sips, he thought that perhaps his mouth would function properly again.

"Nikutsegi," he said. *"Ayuh Nikutsegi.* Tell the Catchers that I'm here."

"That's Nickajack," said someone speaking English. "They're going to hang him in the morning."

"I'll go get the Catchers," said another in Cherokee.

Nickajack sipped at the coffee. It felt good, and it helped some to warm his cold insides, but he felt a sickness in his lungs, a deep chill that seemed to have settled in for good. But the hot cup warmed his hands, and his face seemed to have thawed. His feet were terribly cold though, and the numbness had gone away so they were hurting. People were gathered around him, but he had not yet really seen any of them. He was simply aware of them, aware of their presence. He took another sip of the hot coffee, and he heard the sound of the door opening behind him and felt a blast of the cold winter wind. He heard the sound of stamping feet as men entered the room. He heard one of the men expel a whistling sound of relief.

"Oh," said the whistler. "It's so damn cold out there. Oh, excuse me my language."

"This is Nickajack," said someone in the room. The two Catchers walked over to stand one on either side of Nickajack.

" '*Siyo, Nikutsegi*,'" said one of the Catchers.

" '*Siyo*,'" said Nickajack.

"What happened to you?"

"I fell off my mule while I was crossing the river," said Nickajack.

"From your house?" said the Catcher, his voice incredulous. "To the east?"

"Yes," said Nickajack.

"The Illinois River?"

"Yes."

"It's swollen right now, and it's icy."

"There was no other way," said Nickajack. He sipped at the coffee. It had cooled enough so that he could drink it faster, and he took a gulp. It warmed his insides a little more. Still the deep, sick cold lingered in the lining of his lungs.

"I would have waited for the river to go down," said someone.

"I couldn't wait," said Nickajack. "The time for me to be here is in the morning. I had to come today."

Then someone else spoke to the Catcher standing to Nickajack's right side, the one who spoke in English.

"He's lucky he didn't freeze to death. He made himself sick for sure."

"He won't mind for long," said the Catcher. "Are those his wet clothes?"

"Yeah."

"Can you get them dried out by morning?"

"Yeah."

"Can we stay here tonight? Do you have room?"

"You mean the three of you?"

"Us two and the prisoner," said the Catcher. "The Cherokee Nation will reimburse you."

"Yeah. I've got room."

"Good. We'll stay the night then."

"All right," said the man who was obviously the

proprietor of the tavern. "You two want some coffee?"

"Sure," said the Catcher.

"You, Nickajack," said the proprietor. "You want some more?"

"Yes," said Nickajack. "Thank you," and he handed the man the cup.

As he took the cup from Nickajack, the man shook his head slowly.

"I still don't see why you made that trip on a day like this."

"It was time," said Nickajack.

The door opened again, and another blast of damp, cold air swept the room. The door was slammed shut, and Nickajack heard the voice of the newcomer behind him.

"I'm looking for Nickajack."

He turned to see Coffee Soldier standing there.

"Coffee," he said. "You followed me?"

"Of course," said Coffee, rushing across the room. "What has happened to you?"

"I lost my mule in the river," said Nickajack. "I almost drowned and froze."

"I found the mule," said Coffee.

"I hope you will take him home."

"Of course."

"But how did you manage?" said Nickajack. "The river is bad today."

"I'd probably have gone in the same as you did,"

said Coffee, "if I didn't have my saddle. Even so, it was a very rough crossing."

Someone brought Coffee Soldier a cup of coffee. He took it with thanks.

"This is your friend?" said the man.

"Yes," said Coffee. "For all of our lives."

"He's a strange one to have come in here today just so they can hang him."

"He's an honorable man," said Coffee Soldier. "He's the best man I have ever known."

CHAPTER 17

The day was cold, but the ice storm had passed in the night, and it was not so cold as it had been the day before. Nickajack's hands were tied behind his back. He wondered why they felt the need to bind him. It had been a year since the sentence was passed, and he had been released on his honor, and he had returned. He had returned exactly on time, in spite of the weather and the difficulty of the journey. Yet they had tied his hands behind his back. Two Catchers led him to a wagon, and they helped him up into the wagon bed. It had no tailgate, and Nickajack sat on the back edge, his legs dangling off behind, his eyes looking back where he had been. He felt a sickness deep within his lungs. It must be from the cold, he thought. From falling into the cold water and breathing the cold air. He also thought that he could feel a chill inside his

bones. He had never been so cold. He had never felt
so sick. He thought that it was probably a killing
sickness, and the thought almost made him smile.
Two more Catchers came to the wagon, and the
judge. They all climbed in. Others had gathered
around, and when the wagon started forward with a
lurch, a large crowd followed it along. It moved
south for a ways, then turned west. The crowd following seemed to get larger all along the way.

Nickajack looked out over the faces of the crowd.
Many of them were unfamiliar to him, but he did
see among them the faces of Colonel Walker and of
Coffee Soldier. For a moment he wished that he had
not insisted that his wife remain at home, but he
knew that he had been right in the first place. She
could not have left the children, and he did not
want them to see him go this way. He did not want
his wife to see it either. He was glad, though, to see
the faces of Colonel Walker and Coffee Soldier. He
was glad, after all, that Coffee had come along behind him. It was good to know that right up to the
end one had friends. The wagon was pulling up a
hill, and Nickajack felt like he would fall out on his
face. He had to throw his weight back to feel secure.
Then the wagon turned, once again headed south,
and it was on level ground.

For an instant Nickajack's eyes looked into the
eyes of Coffee Soldier, his lifelong friend, his closest
friend, and he saw there in just that fleeting moment

desperation, hopelessness and wild distraction. He
wished that he could talk to Coffee for just a few
minutes. He wished that he could tell him not to
worry, that life would go on. He longed to be able
to offer Coffee some comfort, but he knew that if he
had the opportunity, he would really have nothing
more to say than good-by. He had had the chance
the day before. He could have talked to Coffee back
there in town, but he had not. He had not done so
in one entire year.

The wagon stopped, and Nickajack looked
around. They were stopped beside a small cemetery.
They must not want to have to haul his body very
far, he thought. He could see some of the stones
clearly. They were mostly made of native sandstone.
Some had letters scratched on them in English,
some in Cherokee. He wondered if someone would
mark his grave with a stone, and if so, what would
be written there. He regretted that he had never
learned the system of writing that Sequoyah had
given to the Cherokees, and it occurred to him that
even if someone did mark his grave with a stone, he
couldn't read the writing. He couldn't read it no
matter which language was used, and, of course, he
wouldn't be around to read it anyway.

The two Catchers seated beside him stood up and
pulled him up to his feet there in the wagon bed,
and only then did he notice that they had stopped
beneath a large tree, and that from a branch of that

tree a rope was dangling with a noose at its end. So this was the place. He stood straight, trying to retain as much dignity as he could. One Catcher held him steady while the other placed the noose around his neck and snugged it down, adjusting the big knot until it was tight against his head just behind and below his right ear. Then the Catchers jumped down out of the wagon. Everyone else had gotten out of the wagon except one man who still sat on the seat and held the reins. Coffee Soldier had pushed his way to the front of the crowd and stood just in front of Nickajack. Nickajack looked down, and he could see the tears running down Coffee's cheeks.

"Good-by, old friend," said Nickajack.

One of the Catchers pulled a piece of paper out of his pocket and unfolded it. Then he started to read. He was reading in English. Nickajack could probably have understood it had he chosen to pay attention and concentrate, but he did not. He wondered how many of the people in the crowd were Ross people and considered him their enemy. He wondered how many of them were waiting there anxiously to watch him die. The English words came out short and choppy, seemingly frozen by the cold air. Nickajack felt like a giant shiver was building up inside him, trying to come out in one big, violent shudder, but it did not. It remained inside with the rest of the chill. He felt consumptive and he wondered if warmth would come with death. The voice stopped, and there was a pause. Then another voice started reading in Cherokee. Still Nickajack did not pay much attention, but he heard enough of it to realize that it was the paper which made what they were about to do a legal action.

The readers finished, refolded their papers and put them back into their pockets. The Catcher who had read the Cherokee looked up at Nickajack.

"Do you have anything to say before we carry out the sentence?" he asked in Cherokee.

Nickajack looked at the Catcher. He looked at Coffee, whose tears still ran freely.

"No," he said. "Nothing. It's time now."

There was a sudden lurch of the wagon, and Nickajack lost his balance. He staggered. He felt awkward and foolish there high above the gawking crowd. He had not anticipated this. The embarrassing moment seemed long and drawn out to Nickajack. Time seemed to slow down almost to a stop. The floor beneath his feet moved forward, and still he staggered. His face began to burn with humiliation there in the freezing air. He felt the soles and heels of his shoes drag and scrape along the wagon bed, and then there was nothing beneath his feet, and he was swinging down and toward the crowd. He was spinning, and he could see the horrified and fascinated faces in the crowd looking at him as he spun. He felt his own weight pulling at him, and he felt the rope tightening around his neck. He couldn't breathe. He could tell that his face was distorted from the pressure, that his features were twisting into grotesque shapes. He started to slobber and drool. He felt a loosening in his guts, and he was afraid that he would foul his trousers. Then he became aware that he was making noises, gasping, gagging, choking noises, noises like a grunting animal.

"They've botched it," he heard someone shout.

Suddenly Coffee Soldier jumped forward, throwing his arms around the shoulders of Nickajack, raising his own feet off the ground and thrusting downward with his own weight until he heard a deathly snap, until he heard no more gagging noises, until he felt no more twitching from the body he embraced, until he knew that Nickajack was dead. Then he stepped back and looked with amazed horror at what had been his friend, and he dropped to his knees, and an agonized wail came out from deep in his lungs to slice the icy air and send new chills up the spines of all the crowd that watched and heard.

Epilogue

It was still cold in the Cherokee Nation, but it was no longer bitter cold. The sun was high and bright in the sky, and everywhere around the ice was melting. It was falling in the form of cold, clear drops of water from the branches overhead. Israel Gunstock and his wife *Aky* were walking along a secluded lane in Park Hill. They had just come from the home of Principal Chief John Ross where they had been royally entertained. Israel was a man perhaps forty years old. His hair was streaked and flecked with gray which served to set off with dignity his finely chiseled full-blood features. He wore a white silk shirt with lace collar and cuffs underneath a tasteful conservative gray suit. *Aky* was dressed in a fit manner to walk beside her husband. She wore a dress and shawl which would have fit right in the high society circles of New Orleans or even Chicago.

They were not in a hurry. They strolled along the lane enjoying the warming weather and each other's company. Life had not been easy for the Gunstocks, but now, even after the bitter Trail of Tears, things were suddenly looking up for them in the new Cherokee Nation. They had established a store at Park Hill and built themselves a comfortable home within easy walking distance of Chief Ross. They counted among their close friends some of the most influential people in the Nation. They had become respected citizens. Only their modesty prevented them from saying "prominent." Although they had not yet reached the point where they would consider themselves to be wealthy, they did feel like they were well on their way, and they both felt sure that it would not be long before they would reach that plateau. And now there was talk that there would likely be a governmental appointment for Israel, possibly even the post of National Treasurer. Chief Ross himself was the source of the talk. He had not said anything direct about it, but he had hinted, and others who were close to the Chief had whispered statements to both Israel and *Aky* that were more direct. *Aky* held her husband's arm close to her as they walked along the lane. She was proud of him, and that pride was reflected in the expression on her face.

"I almost feel guilty," said Israel.

"Whatever for?" said his wife.

"So many people suffered. So many died along the way, and their families are still suffering the loss. Who would ever have thought that out of so much suffering good would result? And why was I chosen to benefit from it all?"

"Don't feel that way," said *Aky*. "We suffered too. But we endured, and now we're prospering. That's nothing to be ashamed of. It's nothing to feel guilty about. Chief Ross says that after all we've been through, all of us, we have to rebuild the Nation. That's what we're doing. That's what you're doing, Israel, and I'm proud of you."

Israel smiled and patted his wife lovingly on her hand, the hand that was holding tight to his right arm.

"Well," he said, "I suppose I can console myself with that thought, and with the thought that even if I don't deserve all this good fortune, you do. I'm doing it for you and for our children."

"For all of us, Dear," said *Aky*. "For the whole Nation."

They walked along a few more steps in silence. Soon they would be home. The lane followed the path of a creek, and just around the next curve, they would see their house. Just then Coffee Soldier stepped out of the bushes. He stood facing the Gunstocks, stood in the middle of the lane blocking their way. The look on his face was frantic, wild, and in his left hand he held the old .46 caliber

Kentucky flintlock pistol that had belonged to Nickajack. His thumb pulled back the hammer and he raised his left arm to point the weapon at Israel Gunstock. Israel raised his left arm out in front of him and opened his lips as if to speak. *Aky's* grip on her husband's arm tightened. She screamed.

"Murderers," shouted Coffee Soldier, and he pulled the trigger. The old pistol flashed and barked, and the lead ball tore its way into the chest of Israel Gunstock. Israel staggered backward. His body went limp and started to sag, its dead weight pulling *Aky* down as she still clutched the right arm. Coffee Soldier stood for a moment, transfixed by the sight of what he had just done. Then he turned and fled. *Aky* sank down on her knees there beside the body of her husband. The murderer's face was firmly etched in her mind. She would never forget it.

This was not the end.

ABOUT THE AUTHOR

Robert J. Conley is a Western writer and editor who specializes in Cherokee lore. He is the author of several novels, including *The Way of the Priests, The Dark Way, The White Path,* and *The Way South.* He received a Spur Award from the Western Writers of America for his 1987 short story "Yellow Bird." In 1992, *Nickajack* received a Spur Award for Best Western Novel of the year. Mr. Conley lives in Tahlequah, Oklahoma.

Robert J. Conley presents the Native American experience as few writers can. Following the success of his award-winning novel, *Nickajack*, Conley has looked back to the early heritage of his own Cherokee people to fashion a remarkable novel about a way of life that will soon be changed forever. . . .

THE WAY OF THE PRIESTS

In the days before the coming of the Europeans, the Cherokees found themselves caught in a struggle for their very survival. The priests, originally responsible only for conducting the religious rites, have gradually extended their control to virtually every aspect of tribal life. Then the Cherokee lands are drained by the worst drought in memory, and the priests, more concerned with preserving their incredible power, are unable to produce the rain necessary to keep their people alive. The priests must take unprecedented steps if they hope to forestall a public uprising. But regardless of what is done, life among the Cherokees will never be the same.

Turn the page for a preview of THE WAY OF THE PRIESTS, a Bantam Domain paperback available in June 1994.

ONE

Saloli, the gray squirrel, must have heard the approach of the children, for he stopped his chattering and sat still on the oak tree branch. He was watching, a picture of total caution. On the ground, maybe thirty paces away, the three children stopped. They were big children, of an age when their childhood was almost over. They would not be children much longer, and probably they knew that, and that knowledge made them play all the more and all the harder at being children while they were still able. Of course they looked forward with eagerness to the responsibilities and the respect of adulthood, to the imagined pleasures of maturity, but they were at the ambiguous time of life when the forward-looking eagerness was balanced with a tenacious clinging to the joys of childish irresponsibility.

The one in the lead was a girl, *agehyuja*. Her name was Selu Ajiluhsgi, or Corn Flower, and she was not only physically ahead of the two boys, her companions, but she was also clearly the leader of the trio. It was she who had seen the squirrel, had signaled a halt to the march and had called for silence. Two paces behind and to her right, Tsisquaya, Real

Bird or Sparrow, watched with unconcealed admiration as Corn Flower slipped a thistledown tufted honey locust dart into one end of her long cane pole blowgun. Already one squirrel had fallen to her deadly aim, and it was hanging limp from a cord around her waist. Sparrow had two, and the third member of the party, Gule, Acorn, standing on a line with Sparrow but to Corn Flower's left, had one.

As Corn Flower slowly raised the gun toward her lips, Sparrow saw out of the corner of his eye Acorn quickly load his own gun and take a too fast shot. The squirrel screamed out in anger, surprise and pain as the sharp dart buried itself in his thigh. He jumped and twisted on the branch, biting at the dart, and then Corn Flower fired a clean shot to the head, and the squirrel dropped.

"Good shot," said Sparrow. He ran toward the prize only a stride behind Corn Flower. Acorn sauntered along at a pouty pace.

"Now everyone but me has two," he said. His chin was practically on his chest, and his lower lip protruded. Sparrow glanced back and noticed how Acorn's hips were swinging heavily from side to side as he walked. He had only recently observed his friend's effeminate characteristics, and he was worried about him. One day he had gone home after play, and he had told his mother.

"Gule acts like a girl sometimes," he had said.

Gatuhnlati, Wild Hemp, his mother, had looked thoughtful for a moment before answering.

"I hadn't thought about it before," she had said, "but since you mentioned it, I guess I have noticed. He has no father, you know, and even worse, his mother has no brothers, only sisters. He's been around women and girls most of his life. I guess he doesn't know how else to act."

"He plays with me," Sparrow had said, "and I don't act like that."

"Of course you don't," she had said, "but the biggest influence is at home."

So Sparrow had decided to spend as much time with Acorn as he could, and anytime he was around Acorn, he exaggerated his masculine manners. He intended to show Acorn by example how young men should behave. Of course, Corn Flower was almost always along, but even her manners were less effeminate than were Acorn's. Sparrow worried about Acorn. There was not much childhood left. He didn't like to think of Acorn as a grown man with the characteristics of a woman. If Acorn was going to change, it would have to be soon. But pouting there over the dead squirrel, Acorn did not show much promise.

"Even the girl's got two," said Acorn. "But not me. Oh, no. I have just one."

Corn Flower had just plucked the second dart out of the warm, soft body. She gave Sparrow a quick glance, and he thought that she read in that instant on his face all that he was thinking.

"This one is really yours, Acorn," she said. "You shot it first."

She held the squirrel by its tail out at arm's length toward Acorn. He took it without a word and tied it to his belt. Sparrow was ashamed for his friend.

"I think we should go back to Ijodi," he said. "We should take these squirrels to our mothers."

"Yes," said Acorn. "I'm tired anyway. This isn't fun anymore."

They turned and started back toward Ijodi, the town where they all lived, and they walked slowly and in silence. Acorn's poutiness had dampened the spirit of fun that had previously dominated their day. Sparrow did not really want the day to come to an end, even though he had made the suggestion. This problem with Acorn was a frustrating one. His example did not seem to be having any effect. He walked slowly and fell behind his two friends. They were all growing up. He was afraid that he would not like the way in which Acorn would mature. But Corn Flower. It suddenly struck him that Corn Flower was already beginning to look like a woman, and she was going to be a very beautiful woman. Just then she stopped and lifted a hand.

"Listen," she said.

Acorn stopped still, his eyes wide.

"What is it?" he said.

"Shh. Someone's coming."

The lane they were on wound its way through thick woods, so they could not see very far ahead. They were well within the vast domain of their own people, *Aniyunwi-ya*, the Real People, and, in fact, they were not far from their own town of Ijodi, so there was no real reason for fear. Rather, it was a childish game they played.

"Come on," said Corn Flower in a loud whisper. "Let's hide and see who it is."

She led the way off the road and into the woods, where the three of them crouched low behind some thick brush. They waited in silence, their hearts pounding almost as if they had been deep in enemy territory. The footsteps came closer. They were heavy footsteps of a big man with a long stride. Then he came in view, and they saw the long, colorful feather cloak flapping behind him as he moved along. They saw the feather crown on his shaven head. And they knew who he was. They crouched still, their fear becoming a bit more real, the play taking on at last a slight element of real danger. He was the single most powerful authority among all of the towns of the Real People. He was a figure who inspired awe and dread among all, wherever he went. And he was seldom seen. Soon he had walked on by. The three companions stood up and moved uneasily back out into the road.

"That was Astugataga, wasn't it?" said Sparrow.

"Yes," said Corn Flower. "That was Standing-in-the-Doorway, the Real Priest, the headman of *Ani-Kutani*, the priests of Anisgayayi."

"I wonder where he's going?" said Acorn.

"He's headed back to Anisgayayi, Men's Town," said Corn Flower. "It's back that way."

"He might be going somewhere else," said Acorn. "You don't know for sure that he's going to Men's Town."

"All right," said Corn Flower. "Let's find out."

"How?" said Acorn.

"You mean follow him?" said Sparrow.

"Yes," said Corn Flower. "Well, not exactly. We'll cut through the woods and get ahead of him. I know some high rocks where we can sit and watch him. Come on."

Again she led the way. It was just habit. She made the decisions. She led and they followed. It had been that way for about as long as Sparrow could remember. He didn't object. It was just the nature of their personalities that caused the behavior. He liked her company, and he liked the adventures into which she led them. He wasn't sure about Acorn's reasons for following along. Perhaps Acorn simply didn't have any other real friends. But Corn Flower plunged into the woods, and Sparrow and Acorn followed without question or comment. For a while all they had to do was dodge around trees and make their way through or around underbrush, but soon they were climbing as well. The going got rougher and steeper. Still Corn Flower kept up a rapid and steady pace. Sparrow was just behind her, but Acorn was falling farther behind with each stride.

They splashed across a swift-flowing mountain stream, and Acorn slipped and fell, skinning his elbow. He started to grow angry, but he scrambled to his feet and ran after his friends, the wet, dead squirrels flapping against his thigh. Then the way grew steeper yet, and they were no longer running uphill, they were climbing. At last, panting and still angry, Acorn was startled when he came right up on Corn Flower and Sparrow sitting behind a large boulder. He scowled, but he pulled himself on up beside them and sat down.

"Why are we waiting here?" he said.

"Look down there," said Corn Flower, pointing around the boulder. Acorn pulled himself up with a groan and moved to look. They were high up above the road, and from their vantage point, they could see a good long stretch of the way below. "We'll see him when he comes along here," Corn Flower concluded. Acorn sat back down.

"If we're just going to wait," he said, "you didn't have to try to run off and leave me behind."

"I didn't mean to run off and leave you," said Corn

Flower. "I thought you could keep up. You're a good runner."

"Besides," said Sparrow, "I was in between. I could see you the whole time. And here we are. All three of us."

"Well," said Acorn, "where is Standing-in-the-Doorway?"

"He'll be coming along soon," said Corn Flower.

"Unless he's already gone by," said Acorn.

"We took a shortcut," said Corn Flower, "and we ran. He hasn't been by here yet."

"Maybe he's invisible," said Acorn. "A *kutani* can do that. He can do that and lots of other things. Maybe he turned into an owl, and he's flying back to Men's Town. We could wait here all night and never see him again."

"He's coming now," said Sparrow, and the other two jumped up to watch around the boulder. Standing-in-the-Doorway had not slowed his pace. He moved in long, quick strides, not looking anywhere except straight ahead. The youngsters stared in awe at the figure of dread moving along there below them.

"Let's go home," said Acorn.

"You go if you want to," said Corn Flower. "I'm going to follow him and watch him go into Men's Town."

"What if he catches us?"

"He'll cook us and eat us if he catches us," said Corn Flower, "but he won't catch us. We'll be careful."

"She's just saying that," said Sparrow. "Come on. He won't do anything to us."

They started down the mountainside toward the road again. Standing-in-the-Doorway had already passed beyond the range of vision from up by the boulder. From that, Corn Flower reasoned, he would be far enough ahead of them by the time they got back down on the road that he wouldn't know he was being followed.

"Just before he gets to Men's Town," she said, "there's another bend in the road. From there the road is straight. We can get to that bend, and then we can watch him go into the town."

"Is there some special ceremony when Standing-in-the-Doorway returns?" asked Sparrow.

"I don't know," she answered, "but we'll find out, won't we?"

They hurried down the mountainside, and although the way was steep, even Acorn managed to make it to the road without taking another tumble, but by the time he got there, Corn Flower was well ahead of him. He trotted along to catch up. At last, at a place where the road curved sharply to their right, she called a halt again. Coming up not far behind her, the boys could tell, even though they couldn't see the road beyond the curve, that up ahead was a deep valley. Down in that valley was Men's Town. They ran up to stand beside her, and just as they arrived, he appeared. They would talk about it later, and they would all agree that they had not seen him walk around the bend or out of the woods. He had simply appeared, standing there before them. His hands were on his hips, and he was looking down at them with a stern, even fierce, expression on his tattooed face. He was easily the tallest man any of them had ever seen—Standing-in-the-Doorway.

"You've been following me," he said, and his voice was deep and resonant. "Why have you been following me?"

If Corn Flower was afraid, she didn't let it show. She stepped boldly toward Standing-in-the-Doorway.

"We have a gift for you," she said. "We brought you these five squirrels."

She pulled the squirrel loose from the cord at her waist, and she turned toward her companions, holding out her hand. The boys jerked loose their squirrels, and Corn Flower took them. Turning back to face Standing-in-the-Doorway, she held out the offering. The big man looked at one young face after the other. One half of his mouth twisted into a wry smile.

"What are your names?" he said.

"I'm called Corn Flower. I'm one of *Ani-Kawi*, the Deer People, and these are my friends, Acorn and Sparrow. They're both *Ani-Tsisqua*, Bird People."

"And where do you live?"

"We live in Ijodi," she said.

Standing-in-the-Doorway reached out to take the squirrels.

"You had better go home," he said. "It will be late now by the time you get back, and your mother will be wondering about you."

Sparrow was frightened, but he had noticed something which was strange, and it was puzzling him. The *kutani* seemed only to look at Acorn, and it was a strange look, a look which Sparrow could not define. The three adventurers had not responded to the suggestion made by the high priest. They just stood seemingly mesmerized. Standing-in-the-Doorway spoke again, this time sharply.

"Go," he said.

They turned and ran. They ran as if their lives depended on their speed, and they ran until they could run no more. At last Corn Flower stopped running and stepped off the road to lean back panting against the trunk of a large oak tree. The boys stopped too. Sparrow sat on a large flat rock, and Acorn just dropped to the ground, falling over on his back. It was some time before they could catch their breath and speak again.

"Well," said Sparrow, "at least he didn't cook us and eat us."

"Corn Flower just made that up," said Acorn. "The *Ani-Kutani* don't do things like that."

"If we hadn't had squirrels to give him," said Corn Flower, "he might have taken us."

"You're just saying that," said Acorn. "You're always saying crazy things."

Sparrow glanced at Acorn. The pout was back on Acorn's face, and Sparrow thought again about the way Standing-in-the-Doorway had looked at Acorn. He wondered if Acorn had noticed that look and, if so, what he was thinking about it. Corn Flower stood up straight.

"Are you ready?" she said. "Let's go."

The boys followed her back onto the road, and they started moving again toward home, but this time they walked. Acorn kicked up puffs of dust deliberately as he walked.

"We didn't even see Men's Town," he said.

TWO

Ijodi had been built beside the river they called Tanasi. When they spoke to it ceremonially, they called it Yunwi-Ganahida, or Long Person, and they knew him as a man with his head resting in the mountains and his feet reaching to the lowlands, and they said that to those who could understand his language he was constantly speaking. Up above Ijodi, not far, was the creek called Sudagi. Perhaps two hundred and fifty people, Real People, lived in Ijodi in houses made of sticks and plastered with mud. The houses were rectangular in shape, perhaps four paces by five paces, perhaps a little larger. Beside each house stood an *osi*, or hot house, much smaller and dome-shaped, also plastered with mud. The side of Ijodi away from the river was lined with small family plots owned, as were the houses, by women, and one large communal garden. In these gardens grew several varieties each of corn, squash, pumpkins, gourds and beans.

The town itself was constructed around a large plaza, and the nearest buildings to the plaza were public, the largest of those being the townhouse. All of this, except the gardens, was enclosed by a palisade fence which, like the houses, was plastered with mud. There was no gate at the entrance; rather the two ends of the fence were deliberately constructed so that they did not meet but ran parallel to each other for several yards, forming a long and narrow passageway through which people could only pass comfortably in single file. As the three wandering younsters returned home, Corn Flower was the first to enter the passageway. Sparrow followed her, and Acorn plodded along in the rear. He was still sullen.

The sounds of shouting and laughter filled the town, and they were coming from the plaza. Corn Flower picked up the pace and led her two loyal followers to the center of town. It seemed as if all of the men and children and some of the women were gathered there. The *gatayusti* game was in progress.

"Let's watch," said Corn Flower, and she ran to the edge of the playing field. Da-le-danigisgi, Hemp Carrier, Sparrow's mother's brother, was just about to make his toss. Bets were still being made by some of the bystanders. Hemp Carrier held in his left hand a polished stone disc, the diameter of which just about equaled the distance from Hemp Carrier's wrist to the tip of his middle finger. The rims of the stone were rounded, and it was concave on both sides. In his right hand he held an eight-foot-long pole, sharpened on one end like a spear. Standing next to Hemp Carrier was Yona-equa, Big Bear, the father of Sparrow. He held a pole in his right hand similar to the one Hemp Carrier held.

Then Hemp Carrier drew back his left arm, swung it forward and with a mighty toss released the stone disc. No sooner had he released it than he began to run after it, the pole drawn back over his shoulder ready to fling. The stone hit the ground some distance ahead and began rolling like a wheel, and Hemp Carrier threw his spear. He stopped to watch its flight. The stone wheel slowed, wobbled and fell on its side, and the spear reached the end of its trajectory about the same time, stabbing itself into the soft ground just ahead of the stone. It fell back then, coming to rest on top of the disc.

A general shout went up from the crowd, and the men who had bet on Hemp Carrier began happily collecting their winnings: arrows, knives, furs. Almost anything could be used for a bet.

"No one can beat my uncle, Hemp Carrier," said Sparrow. "He's the best in Ijodi at *gatayusti*."

"You're always bragging," said Acorn.

Sparrow felt the skin on his face grow hot. He really didn't think it was bragging to express pride in the accomplishments of someone else, and even though his uncle was a winner, it was his father who had lost. Still, he decided not to respond to Acorn's remark. Acorn was pouty and sullen enough already.

"Do you know anyone who can beat Hemp Carrier?" asked Corn Flower.

Acorn pretended not to hear.

"I have to go home," he said, and he turned and walked away without another word.

"What's the matter with Acorn today?" said Corn Flower.

"I don't know," said Sparrow. "I'm worried about him, though. He's my friend, but I don't like the way he's been acting lately. I don't know what to do about it, though."

"There's nothing you can do about it."

"I just try to act right and hope that he notices."

"He's too old, Sparrow," said Corn Flower. "He's already formed his ways. He won't change now."

Sparrow hoped that Corn Flower was wrong, but he didn't say anything more. She was probably right, he thought. He hated to admit it, even to himself, but she was probably right.

*   *   *

Wild Hemp was cooking in front of the house when Sparrow arrived back home. The boy sat down on a short tree stump beside the door to watch her.

"You were out a long time today," said his mother.

"Yes," he answered.

"Were you with your friends?"

"Yes. Acorn and Corn Flower were with me. We hunted for squirrels."

Wild Hemp looked at her son and then looked around as if she were searching for something that should have been there.

"I don't see any," she said. "You didn't bring me any squirrels after such a long day of hunting?"

"No," said Sparrow. "I got some, but I gave them away."

Just then Big Bear walked up.

"I have just lost everything to my brother-in-law," he said. "Now I'm a poor man. I'll have to start all over and make new things."

"That happens to you every time you play against my brother," said Wild Hemp. "You never learn."

"Oh, I don't mind. Besides, he's a challenge for me. I keep thinking that one day I just might beat him."

"Ha," said Wild Hemp.

"Did I hear you asking about squirrels?" said Big Bear, and he looked toward his son. "Did you hunt all day and bring back nothing?"

"I killed two squirrels," said Sparrow. "Corn Flower also killed two, and Acorn killed one, but Acorn was grumbling so, Corn Flower gave him one of hers. I'm ashamed of him, the way he's been acting."

"I've seen him lately," said Big Bear. "He's going to grow up to be a man-woman, I think."

"I've been trying to show him how a man is supposed to behave," said Sparrow, "but it doesn't seem to be doing any good."

"He's nearly grown," said Big Bear. "You can't do anything about it now. Besides, if that's the way he's supposed to be, no one could do anything anyway."

"So where are your squirrels?" said Wild Hemp.

Sparrow sat silent for a moment. Then he told them about the meeting with Standing-in-the-Doorway. He told about the game they played and how they got caught and finally about the clever way in which Corn Flower got them out of trouble by giving away their squirrels.

"I wonder what that *kutani* was doing away from Men's Town," said Big Bear.

"The food is ready," said Wild Hemp. "Let's eat."

She dished out the meal for the three of them, and the conversation came to a halt while they ate venison and beans and squash. When they had finished, they sat back to relax. The sun was already dropping behind the mountains.

"Before the *gatayusti* game," said Big Bear, "I was over visiting with my clansmen, the Blue People, *Ani-Sakonige*. We were talking about the *Ani-Kutani*. Some of the older men said the priests seem to have much more power now than before. Some of them were wondering if it's right."

"There's going to be a big ball play in a few days," said Wild Hemp, adroitly changing the direction of the talk. "Maybe Standing-in-the-Doorway was just out selecting the field."

"That's right," said Big Bear. "That would be his function."

"Who's going to play?" said Sparrow.

"Some *Ani-Chahta* are coming," said Wild Hemp.

"There's a dispute over some land between our towns and theirs," said Big Bear. "*Aneja*, the little brother of war, the ball play, will decide the outcome."

"The winners will own the land?" said Sparrow.

"Yes," said Big Bear. "If the Choctaws win, it will be their land. If the Real People win, it will be ours. It's good hunting land. It's an important fight, so your mother is probably right. Standing-in-the-Doorway was probably selecting the field."

"Or doctoring it," said Wild Hemp, "to make sure we win."

"Where will they play?" said Sparrow.

"Near Kituwah, I think," said Big Bear. "They won't announce the exact site until just before the game. That way the Choctaws won't get a chance to doctor it for themselves. We'll just go to Kituwah on the right morning and wait until they announce the place for the game. Then we'll go out there with everyone else to watch."